ᒫ Sometimes a Stranger

A STACY BELFORD STORY

by Lenora Mattingly Weber

Thomas Y. Crowell Company, New York

Sometimes a Stranger

1 ❧

Y_{OU} can be so happy that you can't sleep, so happy you don't *want* to sleep because you can't bear to let go of the pulsing melody in your heart that hums itself through your lips. It was like that with Stacy Belford at midnight on the twenty-third of December when she undressed in her room at the head of the stairs.

Her soft humming burst into song:

> I only know when *he*
> Began to dance with me . . .

The *he* was a tall, powerfully built boy with broad shoulders, hazel eyes, a thick mat of dark curly hair, and a skin that even in winter never seemed to lose its tan—a boy named Bruce Seerie.

Stacy's younger sister Jill, asleep in the double bed, stirred and gave a throaty rumble. Swiftly Stacy turned out the light and lowered her voice to a croon so as not to rouse the seventh grader. Better her own rhapsodic thoughts than Jill's gab, gab, gab. Yet Stacy's feet kept moving in waltz rhythm all the while she took off her clothes, and put on a short fleecy gown and her blue robe over it. But she didn't take off the heavy necklace she was wearing. It was part of her happiness.

She heard the front door open and close. That must be her older brother Ben coming home from his job at the Ragged Robin Drive-in. It was still a little early for Mother to be returning from her nightly job of playing the piano at Guido's Gay Nineties.

Stacy opened her door as Ben trudged upstairs. The light in the downstairs hall was always left burning for Mother, and against it his tall, lean figure was silhouetted. Ben was the oldest of the six Belford children. He was more than a big brother. Since their father's death six years ago, he had been the watchdog of the family—and the disciplinarian. The Belford children might wheedle any of their desires out of their warm-hearted, impulsive mother, but wheedling had no effect on Ben. His eyes were too wise, his jaw too grim. Mother's No was apt to end up as Maybe; Ben's No never changed.

Stacy said in a whisper, "Did you see the Christmas tree we trimmed, Ben? I left the lights on so you and Mom could see how pretty it is."

"Looks nice," he muttered tiredly. "Did the angel at the top hold together?"

"Didn't you notice it? Bruce patched up the broken wing with adhesive tape."

"Bruce did? Bruce Seerie? Don't tell me he condescended to come in and help trim the tree."

"He certainly did." She was always on the defensive

with her family about Bruce. "We never would have got the lights unsnangled if it hadn't been for him."

"Untangled," Ben corrected automatically. "Better get to bed. It's late."

He went on down the narrow hall to his room. But Stacy wasn't ready yet to wrap up her gladsome evening by crawling into bed beside the warm cocoon that was Jill. She fidgeted about, waiting until the light went out in Ben's room. Then softly she slipped downstairs.

There in one corner of the big room that served as both living and dining room stood the Christmas tree in all its splash of red, green, and amber lights, of tinsel, balls, and striped candy canes. The candy canes wouldn't last long—the littles would see to that. (The three youngest Belfords—the twins, Matt and Jill, and Brian, who was a year younger—were always lumped together as "the littles.")

A big brown and white dog unfolded himself from a corner of the couch where he wasn't supposed to sleep. At Stacy's low "Cully, aren't you ashamed?" he lowered his head and penitently wagged his tail.

Stacy looked musingly at the gossamer angel wired to the very highest tip of the tree. Bruce had patched it up and put it there.

What a wonderful and special evening! It had started when she opened the door for him just as the sun had been dipping down behind the backdrop of mountains to the west. In its light his eyes and hair had looked darker, his face more tanned above his nubbly cream-colored turtleneck.

"Bruce, I didn't expect you so soon," she had exclaimed. "I thought the get-together at your frat house wasn't till seven."

He had come early, he explained, because he wanted to take his mother's and his own Christmas presents out to old Aunt Vinia. "And I have to make another stop first. So how about your coming with me now, and then we'll go on to the party? Well, it isn't really a party, just a sort of farewell-till-we-meet-again doings for those going home for the holidays. Couldn't you get ready right away?"

Jill, all bossy importance, had pushed into the hall. "You can't go yet, Stacy. You promised Mom and Ben you'd help us trim the tree."

"It's the lights," Stacy appealed to Bruce. "They're all so strangled up together."

Bruce chuckled. "You mean either tangled or scrambled." He was well aware from these past two years of knowing Stacy that she herself tangled and scrambled words like no one else. "Maybe I can help unstrangle them."

They had all worked together then on the seemingly hopeless snarl of cords and lights. Some of the lights were little candles with a burble of water in each; some were tapered globes. Matt and Brian hadn't argued with Bruce, the star athlete, but tried to outdo each other in getting the adhesive tape for him to mend the angel's wing, and the kitchen stool for him to stand upon to fasten it to the tip of the tree. Matt, who took pride in his tough-kid image, had even leaped on his bike and broken a speed record going down to Downey's Drug for new bulbs with which to replace the burnt-out ones.

Jill too had tried to impress him. "You're the best Christmas-tree trimmer I ever saw. Have you trimmed your tree at home yet?"

No, Bruce had answered. His mother always hired a decorator to come in and do theirs. This year the tree was to be silver with chartreuse balls on it.

When the Belford tree had been trimmed except for the last final touch of tinsel, Jill had said magnanimously, "We can finish it, Stacy. You'd better get dressed."

Stacy had paused on the second step. "You said it wouldn't be dressy, didn't you, Bruce?"

"Not a bit. It's just one of those drift-in, drift-out affairs."

In her room, Stacy had hesitated in the closet doorway. One ought to wear either red or green for Christmas. But red didn't do too much for a girl with auburn-red hair. She'd wear the Kelly green slip-on she wore for cheerleading at St. Jude's High and a tweed skirt. The skirt belonged to her older sister, Katie Rose, who was most persnickety about anyone else wearing her clothes. But Katie Rose was with her Irish grandparents in the small town of Bannon, fifty-seven miles away; she wouldn't be home until Christmas morning, and what Katie Rose didn't know wouldn't hurt her, Stacy thought as she ran a comb through her long hair and tied it back with a green woven cord.

She and Bruce had set out in the dusk through streets where patches of dirty snow still hugged lawns and curbings. The copper-colored car Bruce drove belonged to his mother. Stacy never felt quite at ease in it because the scent of Mrs. Seerie's perfume—and somehow her presence—lingered in it. And it was Mrs. Seerie, as well as Bruce's father, who didn't approve of Bruce's going with "that redheaded Belford girl."

("They don't like me," Stacy often said to him. And he would answer, "It isn't *you*. They wouldn't like any girl I dated. They've got a thing about my getting involved with any gal before I'm through college and law school.")

They would stop first at Jake's, Bruce had told her, as he turned off busy College Boulevard. He drew up in front of a made-over brick bungalow that had been given a coat of white paint and even in the dusk Stacy could see how the red of the brick showed through the peeling white. "I'll just run in and get the picture he did for Aunt Vinia to cover up a window. His basement rooms are always an unholy mess."

He hadn't needed to run in though. The vacant space next to the house was used as a parking lot, and a man and a girl had been just opening the doors of a rectangular red Volks station wagon. Bruce had honked his horn and called out, "Hey, Jake, hold it. I came to get the picture for Aunt Vinia."

"Coming right up, buster," Jake had called back, and with a loose-jointed, springy stride, made his way through the hedge that separated the vacant lot from the house premises and disappeared.

The girl had come hurrying over to the car then to say with friendly eagerness, "Is this your girl that you're always talking about, Bruce?"

"The only girl I've got. This is Stacy, Allegra."

"I sure am pleased to meet you, Stacy."

"Pleased to meet you." The old-fashioned phrase had held such genuine warmth that Stacy had opened the car door to grasp the girl's outstretched hand. "I'm pleased to meet you too, Allegra."

The light from inside the car had shown her more clearly. What a conglomerate outfit she had worn. Her slacks of imitation leopard skin had been far too short for her long legs, and showed bare ankles and bare feet in white summer sandals. But it had been the coat that Stacy's eyes rested on that somehow stirred a feeling of pity in her. Once, maybe fifteen or twenty years ago, it would have been the sort of dressy coat some middle-aged woman would have worn to a luncheon—a powder-blue, three-quarter-length coat with full sleeves, a tie belt, and—of all things—a yoke.

Allegra's round, country-girl face had been framed by medium-short hair that looked as though she herself had hacked a little off here and there, yet her heavy bangs could have stood trimming. Her radiant, loving smile had made Stacy's heart warm to her.

"Are you going to a party? I dearly love parties," she had said with little-girl rapture.

"I guess you could call it that," Bruce had answered.

Jake had returned then with the rolled-up picture. Without waiting for an introduction, he thrust it at Stacy. "You hold it, sugar—No, not tight enough to mash it, for gosh sakes. And, Bruce, you tell Aunt Vinia I'd come out and paste it onto her window, only I have to take life's stepchild here to Grandpa's Pancake House to see if she can get a job. Just put it over the window—here's some Scotch tape to hold it at the corners—and the first chance I get, I'll be out and glue it on right. And you tell Aunt Vinia I looked at church windows, but I didn't like all those fat, smirking angels with halos, so I did this old boy instead to protect her from the peepers."

Bruce had turned on the motor, but Jake only held on to the open door at Stacy's side. "Don't rush us now, buster. I want to feast my eyes on my understudy. Isn't she a honeypot, Allegra?" And to Stacy, "I understand you pretend to be Jake on the telephone, so's to work a shenanigan on Bruce's bodyguards."

Stacy had flushed. The bodyguards were Bruce's parents. The shenanigan was Bruce's phoning her on Sunday and calling her Jake and asking if they could go over a chapter on International Relations—or some other subject pertaining to college homework—together. Instead, he would pick up Stacy, and they would spend an hour or so together, having Cokes in a corner booth at Downey's Drug, or if the day was sunny, feeding the ducks at the park.

And sometimes Stacy would take malicious delight in slipping something over on Bruce's vigilant parents, and then again she would feel uncomfortably sneaky about what Jake called their shenanigan.

"We've got to shove off," Bruce had said.

But Jake had only continued leaning. His shabby plaid coat hung loose on him. He couldn't have buttoned it if he had wanted to, because all the buttons were off except one that hung by a thread. A lock of lanky brown hair fell over his forehead, and his moustache looked heavy and droopy on his gaunt face. "You can't go yet. I haven't wished Stacy Merry Christmas."

She had laughed at his very brashness.

"There you are, Allegra. We've heard her laugh. Remember this ape-man trying to tell us about Stacy's laugh? He's right. It *is* as contagious as mumps."

Allegra had only stood smiling happily, as though all the world and all the people in it were her friends.

"Now you can go," Jake had added, and taken his weight off the open door.

"He's a cornball," Bruce had said as he swung around the first corner. "But the art teacher at the U thinks he's another Gauguin—or maybe Van Gogh."

"Is Allegra his girl?"

"Oh, not the way you'd think. He helps her out, and she helps him out. She comes in and mucks out that place of his when it gets pretty thick. They don't have dates, if you know what I mean."

"I think she's great."

The dusk had become a gray darkness as Bruce wound through an older residential part of South Denver toward Aunt Vinia's. "I thought your mother put Aunt Vinia in one of those nursing homes."

"She tried hard, but Aunt Vinia dug her heels in." A certain defensiveness always crept into Bruce's voice when he spoke of his mother to Stacy. "You can see what a seedy part of town this is. The old houses are mostly rooming houses or chopped up into apartments with a lot of fly-by-night tenants. That's why Mom worries about her living here alone."

He had stopped in front of a narrow, two-story brick house set in close between two others, which like

Jake's abode had been made into so-called apartments. "When I was a kid, I used to stay with Aunt Vinia when Mom and Dad went off on trips."

Bruce had pressed the doorbell, and a dog inside had set up a high-pitched barking. The door had opened then a narrow crack while wary eyes behind gold-rimmed glasses peered out at them. The wariness turned to pleased amazement at the sight of Bruce with his Christmas packages and Stacy standing beside him. The door swung wide. "Brucie! Isn't this nice—" and to Stacy, "I've been telling him and telling him to bring his girl out to see me. And look at me—such a sight as I am to have visitors!"

From all the talk Stacy had heard about Aunt Vinia's needing to be put into a nursing home, she had expected to meet an enfeebled old woman. But this little lady in her kitchen apron with her flustered apologies about being a sight with her hair in curlers—old-fashioned *kid* curlers, Stacy saw—had been pert and agile.

She had ushered them into what she called "the front room"—a small, cluttered, very warm and stuffy one. Then she had excused herself and the dog. "I'll just be a minute. I was starting to give him his supper, and he'll leave us no peace till he gets it." She had turned back as she went through clinking bead portieres to say defiantly, "And what would I do with little Butch if I let them drag me off to a nursing home?"

Over the rattle of the bead curtains closing behind her, Bruce had muttered to Stacy, "It's the stairs Mom worries about too. And Aunt Vinia's coming down them in the middle of the night to let the dog out. She's fallen on them a couple of times, only she won't admit it."

Aunt Vinia had returned, minus the curlers in her hair. She had carefully unrolled Jake's picture which looked something like a church window done on thin rice paper. It was for the window on her stair landing.

"It used to face the solid wall of the house next door," she had explained to Stacy, while Bruce was putting it in place with the Scotch tape. "Then they made an outside stairway, and folk started traipsing up and down to the second-floor apartment. I thought of getting a stained-glass window, but goodness, gracious, they're so expensive."

They had all stood back to survey the picture. It was of an angular saint with a pointed beard and a look of compassion and wisdom in his eyes.

"Why, that's St. Jude," Stacy had said. "His statue is over the doorway at school. He's the saint of the impossible."

"The saint of the impossible?" Aunt Vinia queried.

"That's right, and Sister Cabrina always tells us if we ask him for something to be prepared for his granting it with an awful wallop." Stacy's laughter spilled out. "Sister says that a cousin of hers once prayed to him for a baby. And guess what she got? Triplets."

A surprising little old lady, Aunt Vinia. With her ruffled apron and veined hands folded in her lap, she had seemed one moment like Whistler's mother. In the next she'd displayed a salty bluntness. "Good," she had answered Stacy with an emphatic toss of her head. "I've

an impossible something to take up with your wal-
loper."

"Go ahead and open the present I brought you, Aunt
Vinia," Bruce had said with a glance at his wristwatch.

Under the Christmas wrappings and ribbon, there
was a timer. "It's the new kind that keeps on ringing.
That's so you won't burn your eggs in the morning
when you go out to feed the birds," he had told her.

"Oh, now. Not every morning. Just when I'm watching those cheeky sparrows so they won't take over the
wren house."

Bruce and Stacy had been unable to leave until
they'd had a drink of grape juice made from the grapes
off Aunt Vinia's arbor. She served it in wine glasses,
and beamed at Stacy's praise. "You forgot to open the
present from Bruce's mother," Stacy reminded her.

"I don't need to." She gave a dismissing glance at the
handsomely wrapped package. "It's bound to be what
we used to call a hug-me-tight; only now they're called
bed jackets. I'll put it with the other three that I've
never worn that she's given me. What's your name
again, dearie?"

"Stacy. I was named after Aunt Eustace—my father's sister. Mom says it really should be Eustacia, but
they're English—and you know how the English give
girls boys' names like Sidney and Leslie, and then
name the boys Evelyn and Beverly."

"How old are you? You look about fifteen."

"Oh, no, I'm going on eighteen."

Bruce had stood up. "We're on our way to a buffet

supper at the frat house, Aunt Vinia. We'd better be shoving off."

"Wait a minute. I've got a present for Stacy."

She had gone upstairs and come back to put into Stacy's hands a green velvet box faded to grayness. "I thought of it when I saw how that green sweater turns your eyes green. Open it."

Stacy had given a gasp of delight as she sprung the catch, and the lid flew back. There lay a necklace of huge uneven greenish-blue turquoises, with streaks and smudges of black and brown, set apart on a heavy silver chain.

"Fifty years ago that Indian jewelry was all the rage," Aunt Vinia murmured. "And somebody told me that heavy jewelry was back in style."

"Oh, it is. And, oh, this is the loveliest I've ever seen. But you—I mean it's too gorgeous. It's too much for you to give me."

"No, indeed, it's not. It's not too much for me to give a girl that Brucie looks at the way he looks at you. And it didn't cost much if that's what's worrying you—not fifty years ago when my husband bought it. Put it on."

"I'll wear it. I'll show it off at the party. And I'll tell everyone it's a present from Bruce's Aunt Vinia."

In a sudden ecstasy that was for more than the present of the turquoise necklace, Stacy had thrown her arms around the donor and pressed her cheek close to Aunt Vinia's warm withered one. It was all so dear, so folksy. It was the first time she had even felt this sort of "family" rapport with Bruce—his pasting up the

St. Jude picture, his explaining about the timer that rang on and on, their drinking grape juice here in this cluttered room with the small dog sniffing at the dog smells on her.

"I feel so Christmasy," Stacy had choked. "So peace on earth, good will to men Christmasy. And so happy I could pop."

"Bless your dear heart," Aunt Vinia had murmured with tears in her eyes.

"Let's go," Bruce had said with typical male embarrassment at this feminine display of sentiment. But he had kissed Aunt Vinia good-bye and said sure, sure, he'd bring Stacy out again. . . .

The sound of the side door opening and closing in the Belford house broke Stacy's bemused reverie. That and her mother's voice exclaiming, "Stacy! What in the world are you doing up at this time of night?"

"I was too wide awake to go to bed. And I wanted to be sure you saw the tree."

2 ∾

H E R mother came into the big room. She slid out of her coat, and gave the convulsive shudder of one coming out of the cold into a warm house. "The Christmas tree. It's lovely. Ah, look at the poor old angel. I never thought it would weather another year."

"It wouldn't have if Bruce hadn't mended the broken wing."

Even as Ben had, Mother exclaimed, "Bruce did? Bruce Seerie? He mended the angel? Will wonders never cease."

And Stacy answered in the same defensive tone, "We never would have got the lights unstrangled but for him."

Mother's face still glowed from the cold night air, but her eyes were heavy and tired. "Would you like some hot tea, Mom?"

"Yes, love, as long as you're still up and cavorting about, stick on the kettle. But undo my dress first."

In keeping with the motif of the Gay Nineties nightclub where Mother played the piano, she was wearing a red satin dress with a stiff bodice and a long full skirt lavishly trimmed with black velvet. She pulled off the black lace mitts that completed the costume and flexed fingers that had romped up and down over the piano keys for hours.

Stacy unfastened the hooks and eyes, leaving only the top one to hold the dress in place, and heard her mother give a long-drawn *ah-h-h* of relief. They both gravitated to the kitchen, where Stacy set the teakettle on the gas. She wished her mother hadn't said that about Bruce. Somehow it dampened her desire to pour out the happenings of her enchanted evening or even to show off the turquoise necklace.

People always told Stacy that she was the "spittin' image" of her mother. They both had the same greenish-blue eyes, the same red hair, and transparent glowing skin. They both laughed readily and heartily, and they both walked as though they were keeping time to music.

As Stacy reached for cups in the cupboard, the necklace, which had been half hidden under her robe, swung out and clinked.

"And will you look at your green beads. Turquoises! And such chunky ones. Where in the world did you get that?"

"Before Bruce and I went to the party, we stopped at his Aunt Vinia's house, and she—"

"Aunt Vinia's house. I thought Bruce's mother had finagled the poor old soul into a nursing home."

"No, siree, she hasn't. Aunt Vinia is still dug in there

with her dog and her grape arbor and now with St. Jude on her stair window. And she gave me—"

"But, honey, real turquoises. She shouldn't have."

"She said Indian jewelry didn't cost very much fifty years ago." Stacy decided not to quote Aunt Vinia's remark about nothing being too much to give a girl that Bruce looked at the way he did at Stacy. "She liked me," she added.

"Then she's the only one of Bruce's family that does," Mother snapped, "the only one who thinks you're good enough for a Seerie. Oh, I know, I know— you've told me often enough that it's because they're afraid their precious son will get involved before he finishes his education. They're afraid something will disrupt all their fine dreams of his being a lawyer and going in with his father." She poured the boiling water into the teapot with a splash. "But it still gravels me. Bruce's mother and her minx coat, as you call it."

(But when Stacy had mentioned the minx coat, Mother had corrected her, "No, it's the minx in the mink coat.")

"I wore the necklace at the party," Stacy said to get her mother off the subject of Bruce's disapproving family. It was a sore spot with Stacy too, but the whole of this enchanted evening, she had thought of it only once, fleetingly, when she had settled herself in the car with the lingering scent of Mrs. Seerie's perfume. She didn't want to think of it now.

Mother stirred milk and sugar into her tea, and took a swallow of it. It seemed to wash down her rancor toward the Seeries, for she said with loving concern,

"Tell me about the party you went to. Did you make a big splurge with your green beads? Was everyone there lost in admiration of you?"

Sweet old Mom. She thought parties were like the ones she used to go to in the little farming town of Bannon when she had been Rose O'Byrne. Stacy knew, because she had heard from other Bannonites, that her mother had had more beaux than "you could shake a stick at," and that whenever she walked into a party, everyone gave a glad shout of "Here's Rose. Now the party can begin."

The party this evening hadn't been that kind. But then neither had it been the kind they gave at St. Jude's when Sister Cabrina always enjoined the girls who were hostesses, "Now remember to make everyone welcome. A hostess never thinks of her own good time but only of her guests. Just remember, Courtesy is to do and say the kindest thing in the kindest way."

Stacy answered her mother, "It wasn't a regular party. Everybody was sort of coming and going."

She remembered how she and Bruce had gone up the steps of what Stacy could see in the dark was a squarish three-story building as two boys came rushing down them. They had stopped, and one had said, "Here's old Bruce in person—he's got a car. You got to go for some rolls." It seemed that someone named Dago had been supposed to provide rolls for the buffet supper, and Dago hadn't shown up.

Bruce had hesitated, but one of the boys took Stacy's arm and said, "I'll take your girl in. You rustle up the breadstuff. Try that delly next to Schmitty's. If they haven't got rolls, get rye—just anything you can find for fillin' food."

The boy had taken her in, shoved her through a wide hall, where couples sat on the stairs with clasped hands and heads bent close together, and on into a huge lounge. Along one side of the room a table had been set with odds and ends of food and a capacious coffee urn. The boy, muttering that he had to check on plane time, had then left.

In the lounge two couples were halfheartedly dancing to some stereo music. A boy in one corner moodily chorded a guitar. One of the dancing couples brushed against Stacy, and she moved closer to the table. No one had said, "Here's Stacy." No one had introduced her to anyone. In fact, no one had paid the slightest attention to her.

A tall slender girl in a white wool dress stood behind the coffee urn. It was an electric one that gave out not a burble but an intermittent belch. The girl commented to Stacy, "Did you ever hear a more nauseating sound?"

Stacy smiled at her. The girl didn't smile back; her eyes were riveted on Stacy's heavy new necklace. "Oh, God, that's the kind I've been trying to find to wear with this dress so it wouldn't look so blah. I've haunted and haunted jewelry shops. Don't tell me you found it in Denver."

Stacy said proudly, "I just got it. It's real old, and it's—"

"Real turquoises. Did whoever you got it from have another one I could pry out of him for love or money?"

"It was a *her*, and it was a present. Bruce's Aunt Vinia gave it to me, because she said it matched my eyes." Stacy's laugh had dwindled almost before it came. For again the girl had not laughed with her. She had only scrutinized Stacy closely for a moment and then turned back to the urn. She held a cup under its spigot and peered appraisingly at the brown liquid.

"It looks done to me," Stacy contributed.

The name of the girl who coveted the necklace had been Joyce. For when Bruce had appeared with his brown paper bag, he greeted her briefly, "Hi there, Joyce." A plump girl in a red jumper that strained across her middle had come bustling in from somewhere then and dumped peanuts, still in the shell, into a dish on the table. Bruce handed her his paper bag. "I had to get Brown-'n-Serve rolls. That's all I could find."

"Oh, wouldn't you know! And I'm not sure how you turn on the oven."

"Maybe I can figure it out," Stacy volunteered.

She had followed the red jumper through another room, skirting a foursome sitting on the floor looking at color slides.

In the kitchen, an embracing couple—both in heavy ponchos—hadn't broken their clinch or noticed their presence when the plump girl shoved against them to get into a low cupboard, not even when she straightened up with a cooky sheet and whacked it against the boy's behind. "Say your fond farewells someplace else, for Pat's sake," she scolded. Very soon, and still with their arms about each other, they drifted out of the kitchen.

While they waited for the rolls to brown, the red-jumpered girl had asked Stacy, "Who's date are you?"

"Bruce Seerie's."

"You are! Well I'll be doggoned."

"Why will you be doggoned?"

"Because Joyce Blackwell—the one in there by the coffee urn—led us all to think she was to be Bruce's date tonight. I must say I think she was a bit obvious, posing in there, waiting for him to show up." She added with dancing malice in her eyes, "Better not drink any coffee she pours you. It might have a drop of strychnine in it."

"You're crazy."

"That's what everyone tells me."

Mother was saying now, "Drink your tea, and we'd better get to bed. Dear heaven, tomorrow is Christmas Eve already, and there's still so much to do. Did you have a nice supper?"

Stacy gave an explosive laugh. "No. It was the goofiest thing. Nothing was organized. There was this big platter of salami and cheese, and somebody brought celery stuffed with cheese, and there were olives—oh, yes, and peanuts with hulls on. And Bruce got all the rolls they had at some little store, but there were only about eighteen. I didn't like to rush up and help myself—but I did grab off a slice of cheese. And then a carful of fellows came in from skiing—five of them. Honest, it was just like the locusts descending. They wolfed down every bit of salami and cheese, and every blessed olive and—"

"Such manners! Did you dance?"

"No, because it wasn't very good music to dance to. One fellow kept playing his guitar, and it was offbeat from the stero. Bruce and I tried to. . . ."

They had been dancing together when one of the skiers, still chomping down one of the Brown-'n-Serve rolls, had tapped Bruce and said, "Can a hardy mountaineer dance with your girl?" But Bruce had only pulled her closer and said, "Not tonight. She's all mine."

"Imagine not getting anything to eat," Mother said aghast.

"Not there. But Bruce asked me if I was hungry, and I said I was starvelous, so we left—by then a lot of them were leaving anyway. And we went to Schmitty's and had one of his corned-beef sandwiches. Bruce's friend Jake was there eating chili."

When they came in, Jake had stood up from a corner table. Waving a brown-coated spoon at them, he had shouted, "Over here, buster. We can all crowd you in." But Bruce had shouted back, "Oh, no. I don't trust you."

Stacy went on. "And Schmitty has all those sentimental records on his juke box. Someone was playing *My Fair Lady* ones. It was fun there. Everybody just cut loose. One fellow stood up and sang 'With a Little Bit of Luck.' A few of us danced in the space between the tables and the counter. And I was singing to 'I Could Have Danced All Night,' and Schmitty's wife asked me—and the kids too kept pounding on the tables and yelling for me to sing it loud enough so they could all hear it—so I did."

Mother laughed. "Oh, sure you did. You're just ham enough to love showing off. So am I, of course."

Schmitty himself had played the record over again for Stacy to sing to. She had not only sung it, but done a soft-shoe dance in three-four time that Mother's brother, Uncle Brian, had taught both Katie Rose and Stacy.

She had sung out, "I could have spread my wings—" and a male voice in the corner had put in, "Spread them over in this direction, cutie."

"And done a thousand things—" "Like what?" had challenged another voice. And when she had reached the "I Could Have Danced All Night," Bruce, who was standing beside her, had taken her in his arms to dance the repeating chorus with her.

Ah, that had been dancing—no fumbling, no missteps. Their four feet had moved in unison, their two bodies had moved as one to the lilting melody.

"Let's dance right out of here," Bruce had said suddenly.

"Bruce, you're not mad because those jokers were wisecracking while I was singing?" Some of their quarrels had been because she was always more gaily outgoing than he.

"No, not that. I just want you to myself. Come on. We'll get our coats."

He had been helping her on with her coat when two women, hatted, gloved, and clutching purses, had wended their way to their vacated table. One had stopped to say, "Why, hello, Bruce." At his blank expression, she added, "I'm Miss Englemann, a friend of your mother's. We just stopped in for a cup of coffee."

The other had said primly, "We didn't expect to see a floor show."

Bruce and Stacy had walked through the stabbing cold of the night to the car. "Who was that woman that spoke to you, Bruce?"

"Darned if I know. Some old biddy that belongs to one of Mom's clubs, I suppose. Said her name was Englemann."

"Englemann. Oh, I know who she is. She's the schoolteacher that lives next door to Claire. You know Claire, my friend at St. Jude's. Claire's mother calls Miss Englemann Ivy, and Claire and her dad call her Poison Ivy."

And somehow the thought of the woman named Englemann had been like a brushing of poison ivy. She was the neighbor who constantly prattled to Claire's folks about the wonderful altruism of Mrs. Seerie with her untiring work in civic clubs. "You'd think to hear her," Claire had said, "that Mama Seerie was Joan of Arc, sent by the angels to save the world."

Bruce had driven through the park and stopped the car close to the small duck pond where they so often came. Tonight, all had been frozen and still, the lake black as shoe polish and rimmed with snow. They had sat in relaxed content, their hands clasped, each soaking up the presence of the other.

Stacy had forgotten completely the other times, the times they had lashed out at each other, and parted in bitterness, only to draw together again with apologies. She had forgotten her rankling resentment against his interfering parents. She didn't even notice the scent of his mother's perfume in the car.

"All this and heaven too," she murmured.

His grasp on her hands had tightened, and he kissed her cheek. But not her lips. There had been a night not long ago in this very spot when a wet-feather snow had enclosed them in this very car. And that night, their long kiss had set up a wild clamor of desire in both of them. It had been jolting, frightening. Since then, Bruce, in something of both fear and protectiveness, had been careful not to "let things get out of hand." And Stacy had loved him the more for it.

"Some day we'll be married, Stacy," he said. He meant, "Someday we won't have to worry about things getting out of hand."

She laughed shakily. "Lawsy me, is this a proposal?"

"Proposal," he grunted. "You know darn well I can't live without you. That I've never looked at another girl."

"Same here."

"Says you. You draw boys like bees draw nectar. What do you know? That's what Jake called you— honeypot." He chuckled. "I used to be jealous and act mean because of the way you drew them."

"But I always got drawn back to you. You're magnetic."

"So are you, honeypot, to me."

Yes, there was no denying the magnetic pull that always brought them together again after their quarrels —even after his long absence when his parents sent him to Nebraska to forget her.

He had fumbled at the knot and untied the cord that held her hair back, till it fell over her shoulders and he could riffle his fingers through it. She broke the long silence with a heavy, "I'd better get home before Ben does. You know how bossy he is."

"Someday we'll be married," he had repeated, and this time he meant, "And then there'll be no Ben to check up on us."

But when he had stopped the car at the Belford house on Hubbell Street and walked her to the door, she had still been loath to say good night. She had talked on just to hold him longer. About how the O'Byrne grandparents in Bannon always came on Christmas morning, about how Gran stuffed the turkey, and how Grandda timed their arrival so it could go into their oven and be ready for dinner around four. "And Katie Rose will come with them, of course. And Liz too—she's one of our relatives. I suppose your folks will have a big Christmas dinner."

The biggest one would be tomorrow night, Christmas Eve, he had said. "Dad calls it Mom's ax-grinding one because she invites business friends of his. She goes all out on it. Then on Christmas Day, she has all the relatives. But I'll be by to say Merry Christmas, maybe between chauffeuring all the ancient kin to and fro." He had kissed both her cold cheeks—and left.

In the Belford kitchen, Mother got up from the table. She picked up her own empty cup and reached for Stacy's. It was still half-full while she sat there dreaming in a rapt faraway haze. Mother said with something of alarm in her voice, "Oh, Stacy love, don't let yourself get so wrapped up in Bruce. Please, child. Because—well, I just can't see any happiness ahead for you."

"You never liked him," Stacy accused.

"That isn't true. I haven't a thing against him. He's a nice, well-mannered boy, but I have a lot against his folks and their looking down their noses at you—at us." This time she couldn't swallow the fury that this thought always aroused in her. She added vehemently, "And he's so completely under their thumb."

"Oh, I wouldn't say that," Stacy flared. Yet she had said it to herself and to Bruce again and again.

"I will say it. They sent him back to Nebraska last year to get him away from you. They never would have brought him back this fall except for his mother's breaking her collarbone. And she's used that as an excuse to keep him tightly tethered."

"Tightly tethered! What else could Bruce do but drive her places when she wasn't able to drive herself? But now she can, and so he doesn't have to. Now he's on his own."

"On his own, my eye! He picks you up after school and drives you home. You can just bet his folks don't know he does it."

That was so uncomfortably true, Stacy couldn't deny it. She could only fling out, "Mom, for heaven's sake, we're not about to elope."

"God forbid. Oh, love, I'm afraid for you and the heartache you're letting yourself in for."

Stacy shoved herself off the dining-nook bench. "Let's go to bed. I'll turn out the Christmas tree."

She walked slowly up the stairs. She wished now she had crawled in beside Jill and taken the melody and rapture with her. She had said to Bruce once, "If there was just us in the world, we could be so happy." It was true. Why did other people have to tarnish the bright gleam? Parents!

3 ❧

T H E Belford family always went to mass at eight o'clock on Christmas morning, so as to be home in good time for the relatives who would drive in from Bannon. This Christmas the service was a folk mass. Stacy had learned the chords, and she crowded herself and her guitar in back of the banked poinsettias with the other young musicians at the side of the altar to play and lead in the singing.

By nine thirty the family was home again, and Ben was sternly admonishing Matt and Brian, "You're not to open a single present till the folks get here."

Mother, drinking a cup of warmed-up coffee, said, "Jill, see that everything is out of the big chair in the living room for Gran because she—"

"I'm lighting the oven," Jill said with preening importance. "Nobody else ever thinks to preheat it for the turkey they bring."

Mother flashed Stacy a look that said, "Sometimes I'd like to wring her neck."

At that, the loaded station wagon with its Bannon license plate pulled up outside the Belfords' picket gate.

Katie Rose was the first to tumble out, her arms piled high with packages. And where Katie Rose went, there went her little blond poodle. He was here this morning, making excited sorties to greet Cully, with the pleased twisting of his body that had earned him the name of Sidewinder, and then darting back to brush Katie Rose's ankles.

Grandda came next. A builder by trade, he had put up most of the schools and dwellings in Bannon. He stood as tall and erect as one of his own two-by-fours, his reddish hair with scarcely a thread of gray. In his younger days he had been with the Abbey Players in Dublin, and he still found time to direct plays in and around Bannon and to act in them.

His Irish brogue always thickened when he was moved by excitement or emotion. This morning he pulled Mother close and called her his dear own. He encircled Stacy with his other arm and wanted to know what she put in her eyes to make them as green as the grass in Armagh.

"Wurra, wurra, and I've been after pushing and prodding the womenfolks all morning to get them and all their bits and pieces loaded in the wagon," he said.

It was from his side of the family—the O'Byrnes—that Mother and Ben and Stacy inherited their red hair. The littles had hair in varying shades of golden brown, somewhat the color of corn flakes. Katie Rose was the only dark-haired one of the six Belford children. Grandda often called her Blackbird.

He turned back to the car now. "Wait a bit till I unload this cripple in the front seat."

"I'm no cripple," Gran corrected briskly. "I can walk as good as the next one."

She had fractured her hip in September. That was the reason Katie Rose had gone to Bannon originally. The reason for her staying on was to take the leading role in the play Grandda had directed and put on.

Gran was a little brown sparrow of a woman whom Stacy had never seen in anything but a button-down-the-front dress that was always too long for her small figure. Mother was forever scolding her about the gawky length and wanting to turn up the hem for her.

The last to heave her plump, bundled-up, rosy-cheeked self out of the back seat was Liz. She was a frequent visitor and one of the Bannon relatives, though the young Belfords could never quite figure out the degree of cousinship. Liz righted herself with an "Ah, there's Stacy—and getting lovelier by the day. And our Brian, the littlest boyeen." She too was loaded with presents—her knitted offerings of bedsocks, scarves, and mittens.

It took the combined efforts of Ben, Stacy, and the littles to carry in the turkey roaster, the mince pies, and the extra provender that always came from Bannon: thick cream in a Mason jar, eggs packed in shoe boxes, and an unwieldy chunk of meat that might be ham or maybe venison. "Poor Rose, and all those hungry mouths to feed," Gran would have murmured all the time she was getting everything together.

And thus the noisy, heart-warming bedlam that was Christmas at the Belfords' got under way. The fragrance from the gifts of perfume and soap mingling with that of roasting turkey and mince pies. The ohs and ahs as presents were opened, the rustle of tissue paper, and the cries of "Get the dogs out before they knock over the tree!" (For by now Sidewinder was enough at home to be playing hide and seek with Cully.) Matt muttering as he opened Liz's present, "More mittens," and Jill reproving loftily, "Do you have to be such an oaf?"

A long florist's box was delivered to Stacy. Killarney roses, and a card, "Merry Christmas, Stacy. Bruce." Her Christmas would have been even merrier if she could have spilled out to them all, "He's the only boy who ever sent me roses, and he says these tawny pink ones remind him of me." Mother said only a tight-lipped "From Bruce, I suppose" as Stacy set the vase of them on the mantel. Gran and Grandda made no comment. Of course, Mother had told them of Bruce's folks looking down their snooty noses at Stacy and her family.

The table for Christmas dinner was set for twelve—ten of the family and two guests. Ben had invited a co-worker from the Ragged Robin. He came early and settled himself on the floor to help Matt and Brian assemble their racing-car set.

Miguel—Katie Rose's beau as Gran called him—arrived in his midget car from the university town thirty miles away. His real name was Michael, but he had come to Denver from a Mexican school with "Miguel" on his transcript and the name had stuck. Stacy remembered the first time she had ever seen him. Goodness, was it three whole years ago? His straw-colored hair still seemed to go in all directions. He still looked as though he had picked up someone else's clothes by mistake, and the same chipmunk grin was in evidence as he handed out his Christmas presents wrapped in sheets of newspaper from the Sunday comics. (Brian carefully collected them all because there were some he hadn't read.)

There was no need for Katie Rose to be defensive about Miguel. He was like one of the family. Stacy thought unhappily of how standoffish Bruce generally was when he called for her at her family's. But last night he had helped unstrangle the lights and patch the broken wing on the angel.

Miguel had pet names for them all. *Mamacita* for Mother, Petunia for Katie Rose, and *Petit Chou* for Stacy herself. (When Stacy first heard it, she had thought he was calling her "petty shoe," instead of "little cabbage.") By no stretch of her imagination, could she picture Bruce throwing his arms around Liz the way Miguel did, or of Liz crooning endearments to Bruce as she did to Miguel, hugging him close in return.

No, and Bruce would never hunker down to poke at the toes of Brian's shoe skates, and pass judgment. "Just a *little* long, but you can put wadded-up cotton in the toes this year, and next year they'll be just right." Nor would Bruce ever say to their guest when he learned that he played the flute, "And you didn't bring it? Well, come on. I'll run you over to your place and get it. We can go there and back in my little bug in two shakes."

Stacy kept wondering what time Bruce would stop by.

Others arrived. Guido, who owned and managed the Gay Nineties where Mother played the piano and sang requests, was the first. He brought his mother with him, and he had a bottle of red wine in one overcoat pocket and a bottle of white in the other. Bruce would never be able to talk Italian to Guido's little black-eyed mother with her skin like a withered apple. But then, Stacy defended him to herself, Bruce hadn't been all over the world with a writer-father the way Miguel had.

Claire, Stacy's best friend at St. Jude's, came running in next. Claire's hair was neither blond nor brunette, but an in-between mousy brown, and it was neither long nor short, so that she caught it back with combs and left it on its own. She wore thick-lensed glasses over eyes that were halfway between blue and gray, and heavy braces on her teeth—"the barbed wire," she called them.

During all of their three and a half years together at St. Jude's, these two had relied on each other. Stacy had need of Claire's down-to-earth common sense and loyalty. Being a far more serious student than Stacy, Claire pointed out to her the subtle meanings and messages in their contemporary literature course, and guided her through the intricacies of algebraic equations. Claire, in turn, basked in Stacy's gaiety and popularity without a tinge of jealousy, and gratefully accepted the dates Stacy wangled for her.

Claire had come partly to exchange presents with Stacy and partly to sputter out her wrath because her orthodontist hadn't taken off "the barbed wire" in time for Christmas. "Him, and his promises!"

If only Bruce would come now, Stacy thought, we could use the excuse of taking Claire home. And then we could ride back together and talk in the car.

But Bruce didn't come. Stacy stepped outside the door with Claire when she left. "Guess who was in Schmitty's last night when I was there with Bruce. That neighbor of yours, Miss Englemann."

"Old Poison Ivy in person, huh?"

"And the woman she was with said something about their seeing a floor show. That meant me, dancing and singing 'I Could Have Danced All Night,' and then Bruce and my dancing together. Do you suppose she'll tell Bruce's folks?"

"I don't *suppose.* I *know* bloomin' well she'll waste no time running to Mama Seerie about it. I can just hear her. She'll lead off by saying, 'I think, as a friend, I should tell you—'"

"Oh, gawd."

"Why doesn't Bruce ever stand up on his hind legs and tell his folks he's out of kindergarten?" Claire said wrathfully as she went down the steps.

A few minutes later, Ben's girl, Jeanie Kincaid, dropped in. She too was like a member of the family. Grandda called her the leprechaun, and there *was* something of elfin charm about a girl with cinnamon-brown eyes who was so small she didn't even reach to Ben's shoulders. Ben called her Mopsy, partly because her hair seemed almost too heavy for her small oval face, and partly because when she was giving serious thought to something, she wrinkled her nose like a rabbit.

(Jeanie had known Bruce Seerie long before Stacy had. It was she who had first told her that he was parent-ridden. And how irate Stacy had been!)

Ben ceased to be the grim watchdog of the family when Jeanie was around. This was the Ben who sang out, "I dream of Jeanie with the cinnamon-brown hair," and whose hearty guffaw was so deep it seemed to come from the soles of his feet. "She's good for him," Mother often said. "I used to worry about his getting old before his time looking after all of us."

Bruce didn't come until dinner was nearly over. Stacy and Katie Rose were clearing away the plates; Liz was cutting mince pies in the kitchen; and Mother was checking to see how many wanted a regular serving and how many a sliver.

Stacy's eye caught the flash of the copper-colored car even before Cully's bark sounded. She plopped down a plate of pie in front of Grandda, and streaked to the door before Bruce had time to ring.

As always there was that first breathless inventory. His eyes raked over her as though to assure himself that her hair was the same glinting auburn, and her eyes as bright and welcoming as when he had last seen her. And she gazed at him to catch the glimpse of white teeth in his tanned face when he smiled and to note his deep broad chest and broad shoulders, which today looked broader than ever under the thickness of a new hand-knit sweater, ecru in shade. She could whiff the leather of the new gloves he held crumpled in one hand.

"We're just on the pie. Maybe—Would you like to join us?" But she said it halfheartedly. In all that melee of people, of food, of dogs underfoot, with the clutter of opened presents and with part of the Christmas tree lights burned out, he would be ill at ease, and Mother would call it uppishness.

He shook his head. "I've still got the ancient relatives to take home. They're all opening presents now, and I couldn't stand it any longer. Can't you come for a ride?"

Stacy's presents were stacked on the piano bench in the hall, and she snatched up a green wool scarf—Liz's present. At the look of inquiry on Mother's and Ben's faces, she muttered that she was going to Downey's Drug with Bruce to get more lights for the tree.

They went to Downey's Drug, almost deserted except for two men who were waiting for the evening paper, and headed for their own special corner booth. They toyed with bottles of Coke. Stacy couldn't find room for more than two swallows.

They talked in an intimate mumble, their heads close together. That is, Stacy talked. She told him about their Christmas. She stretched a point and said that everyone thought his roses were gorgeous. "I wanted to get you something," she grieved, "but I couldn't think of a thing you didn't have."

"I know. The man who has everything." He added with low vehemence, "Christmas. Thank God, it's over."

"What's the matter, Bruce?"

"Let's get out of here," he said in a driven voice.

They got up then and left Downey's Drug, with Stacy giving never a thought to the Christmas tree lights.

Bruce drove aimlessly through the residential streets, empty and deserted as though Christmas held everyone indoors. And he told her, in the short, choppy sentences he always used when he was upset, about the un-merry Christmas Eve and the un-merry Christmas Day in the Seerie split-level house in the exclusive suburb named El Vista.

His mother had invited the guests to come to her ax-sharpening, Christmas Eve dinner at seven. "There's always that party Dad has down at his office. It gets started about three. It's only supposed to last an hour or two. Mom figured he'd be home in plenty of time. You know—genial-host stuff—mix drinks for the folks. . . ."

"Wasn't he?"

"Lord, no. There's this fellow Blackwell that's moved here from Kansas City—he's building a new addition out near Delmar Dam—and he—"

"Blackwell? Is that Joyce's father? Was she there too?"

He nodded. "The ax-sharpening there is that Mom wants Dad to get the legal work. Anyway, Blackwell took over serving the drinks. Then we waited—and we waited. About nine Mom went ahead and had dinner served. Blackwell had to carve the bird too. We were halfway through when Dad showed."

"What in the world had happened?"

"Some gal had fallen at the office party. Name's Louise, I think. She works part-time for the firm. Dad said she was going to leave early because she still had to go Christmas shopping for her two little girls at home. But some bozo—I suppose he'd had a few too many—grabbed her arm and spilled his drink as he did so. At least Dad figured that's what made her slip. Her foot doubled up under her, and she tore a ligament in her ankle."

"Oh-h-h."

"So Dad took her to the hospital. Guess he felt responsible because it happened at his office. He waited for the X rays—you know how long that takes. And for the doctor to put a cast on."

"Just for a torn legament?"

"Not *leg*ament, goon. *Lig*ament. That's as bad as a break. Takes as long to heal too, and it hurts worse. Dad took her home. He said she was more worried about the two little kids not having anything in their socks the next morning than she was about herself. I guess it was a dreary mess at home. The baby sitter sore as all get out. No food. So he went out to scrounge up something to put in the socks and something for them to eat."

Stacy listened in wonderment. It was hard for her to picture Bruce's father, that dapper, cut-and-dried, money-minded man, being concerned about whether two small girls had full or empty Christmas stockings —or full or empty stomachs.

She thought aloud. "Why didn't he bring them home? I mean, your mother could have given them some of the turkey, and—"

Bruce gave a mirthless bark of laughter. "*Turkeys.* Two of them. A big one for last night, and another for the relatives today. No, not Mom. She was sore as a boil anyway because Dad had upset her evening."

"But not after he explained about what happened, for gosh sakes?"

He answered slowly, "She was even madder when she heard what happened. That's the trouble with people that have to have every detail planned to perfection. They go into a tailspin when something upsets their pattern—their beautiful pattern."

"They" meaning his mother. As though Stacy didn't know that the beautiful pattern for Bruce did not include the girl who was sitting beside him. As though Mrs. Seerie hadn't made that plain every time she came within speaking distance of Stacy.

He added flatly, "Even today. It's about as Christmasy and festive at our house as a deep freeze."

That too was hard for Stacy to understand. Her own mother was the kind who exploded and then gave the one she had exploded to a loving pat. Even Ben would lace down the littles when they came home battered and bruised from a neighborhood fight, but the next minute he would be covering their cuts with Band-aids and their bruises with a smelly salve.

She breathed out, "Oh, poor Bruce. Oh, poor everybody at your house."

She could picture it all, though she had seen it only once when she had been invited to Bruce's birthday dinner. Outside, the landscaped swimming pool and the patio with its view of Pikes Peak—or Piker's Peak as Stacy called it. Inside, the wall-to-wall carpeting and interior decorator's arrangement of furniture, pictures, and mantel treatment. Oh, yes, and the silver tree with the luster of chartreuse balls. She shivered under Liz's scarf at the thought of the arctic temperature hovering over all.

Bruce turned the car toward Hubbell Street. He didn't stop outside the white picket gate, but drove on to the next corner where a weeping willow tree dropped its leafless branches. Just as the corner booth at Downey's was their own booth, so was this their own weeping willow. Here they had lingered, reluctant to say good-bye. Here sometimes they had fought bitterly. Here over a year ago they had gone through a final parting—or so Stacy had thought. With the tears rolling down her cheeks, she had sobbed out, "Oh, Bruce, where did the roses go? Why does our willow tree have to weep? . . . We do terrible things to each other."

But always there had been that strange affinity that brought them together again.

She said haltingly, "Bruce, I want to tell you something." She always led off with that when she was unsure of how he would respond. "Maybe you'll laugh—

Oh, I know you'll think it's goofy, but at church this morning. . . ."

She told him then of her playing the guitar accompaniment with the others and leading the singing of the congregation. "At Communion we played that Negro spiritual, 'O Lord, cum ba ya.' It means 'come by here.' And I watched everyone coming up the aisle for Communion. Some looked so old and tired . . . but all the kids in their new coats or boots looked so proud. And some of the fathers and mothers carried babies because they couldn't leave them in the seats. There was one woman who used to sell Avon—you know, 'Avon Calling!'—only now she has arthritis so bad she has to be pushed up in a wheelchair. And all at once I felt so sort of lifted out of myself, and I loved them all so much it hurt inside. Bruce, I couldn't even sing for the lump in my throat. It was just as if He had come by me. Just the way it says in the Bible—as if the hem of His garment had touched me. There!—I guess you think I've got rocks in my head."

He moved closer to her. "No, not that. I think you've got goodness in your head—and all through you. Keep on talking. I can feel the kinks smoothing out. Gosh, I hate to go home."

"But it didn't last," she admitted forlornly. "Not that *cum-ba-ya* feeling. I got so mad at Jill I almost killed her. Imagine her helping herself to my best perfume—there was just a teensy little bit of it left—and dousing it all over herself."

"Tell me something we can both laugh about. I haven't heard a laugh in two days."

Before she could answer, the back door of the Belford house opened. Jill erupted through it and the gate, and came racing toward the copper-colored car. "Wouldn't you know it!" Stacy muttered.

Jill opened the door on Stacy's side, letting in a gust of the looted perfume which temporarily dimmed the lingering scent of Mrs. Seerie's. "I thought I saw you drive by. That friend of Ben's from the Robin is going to play," she announced. "And everybody's going to sing. They want you, Stacy, and Ben and Miguel said for you to come in too, Bruce."

Bruce had ready his excuse of the relatives he must pilot to their doors. Stacy said, "I'll be home in a minute, Jill. Tell them I'll be there in a minute."

Jill raced back through the chill dusk.

For just another moment Stacy wanted to share this small island of the front seat of the car with Bruce under the willow tree's sheltering branches. "Hold my hands, Bruce," she begged.

He yanked off his new Christmas gloves and cradled both her hands in his. She was really saying, "Hold my hands, so I'll feel *we* belong together, even if you don't belong in my house and I don't belong in yours."

4 ⁓

S *T A C Y' S* happiness went with her into the New Year.

The first Monday after the holidays, she, Claire, and Liesel Muehler ate their lunch together as usual in the noisy din of St. Jude's lunchroom. Liesel, with her flowerlike face, was the daughter of a dour and strict German delicatessen owner. She always did the most chattering. Claire said it was because when Liesel was at home, she had to withdraw into a silent shell with the disapproving man she called papa.

Today there was so much to catch up on. Liesel had to show them the scarf Sully had given her for Christmas. (Sully—sometimes called Big Sully to distinguish him from his brothers—was a shy, hulking football player whose real name was Sullivan.) "I have to wrap it around my middle under my skirt when I go home," Liesel said with a pleased giggle, "so Papa won't see it."

"Any takers for fruitcake?" Claire asked. She unwrapped the waxed paper that contained three dark thick slices. "This is all we had left from all the Christmas goodies."

Stacy and Liesel each took a piece. Claire bent over it and took a whiff of the remaining slice. "Citron. And I loathe it. I might have known that woman would be the sneaky type to put citron in fruitcake."

"What woman?" Liesel wanted to know.

"Our gabby neighbor next door."

"You mean Poison Ivy?" Stacy asked.

"Right. Poison Ivy, the dear buddy of Bruce's mother. Honestly, those two trotting off in the Seerie car to all those Save-the-Landmarks, and Keep-Our-City-Clean clubs! And now they've launched an organization to move the migrants out of their unsanitary shacks."

"Where will the migrants go when they move them out?" Liesel asked with her wide-eyed Alice-in-Wonderland air.

"Don't ask me. And don't ask the Move-the-Migrants-Out bunch." Claire laughed with malicious amusement. "You ought to hear Dad bait Poison Ivy. He asked her when she and Mama Seerie were going to find room for the poor migrants in their own homes. That really threw her."

"Did she say anything about seeing Bruce and me at Schmitty's?" Stacy put in.

"Not to me. But I'm sure she passed the word along to the civic leader, the doer of good in the community. You want this other gob of fruitcake?"

"No," Stacy said.

"Say 'No, thank you,'" Claire corrected in a mimicking voice.

"No. No, no-thank-yous. It's lousy fruitcake."

And then Liesel broke in with what Sully had said this morning when they met at her locker, and what she had said. . . .

At the end of school, Stacy went down the worn stone steps of St. Jude's into a misty drizzle that might turn into snow. Her eyes sought the driveway where Bruce always stopped the copper-colored car to wait for her. It wasn't there today.

A boy came clumping down the steps behind her and pulled her close. "Hi, my secret gnawing passion. Want a ride home in the hearse?"

"I'm not sure, Obie."

Just the way Sully was short for Sullivan, Obie was short for O'Brien. He was the slightly built, wiry quarterback on the football team as well as the school comedian. The hearse he referred to had indeed served many years as just that. Obie had bought it cheap, taken out the flat platform on which the coffin used to rest, and fitted in two back seats. They were not a perfect fit and, even weighed down with young passengers, rocked perilously and hilariously every time Obie turned a corner.

Other students were hurrying through the misty rain toward the hearse, Stacy saw. "Have you got room for me, Obie?"

"When there's room in the heart, there's room in the hearse," he said unctuously. But at that very moment, the copper-colored car swirled into the driveway. "Ah, there's your Romeo. 'Twas ever thus. Me and my unrequited love."

"Some other time, Obie," Stacy said, and went winging across the fifty feet of wet lawn to the car and the door Bruce held open for her.

She settled herself beside him and, even as Liesel did, chattered on to get him caught up on everything that had happened since she had last seen him. "Guess what? Katie Rose isn't coming back home to stay this winter, but she will still be here for weekends now and then. So that means I'll still have to share my room with Jill, and that means I'll have to listen to her gab, gab, gab about Itsy Sullivan. He's Big Sully's little brother, and he's in Jill's class at school. It's been quite a dose of Sullivans—hearing Liesel rave on about Big Sully every noon and between classes, and then having Jill spill over about Itsy at home. I used to play baseball with the Sullivan kids on the corner lot, you know."

"Did you say Katie Rose isn't coming back?" he asked absently.

"That's right. She's decided to go to that teachers college that isn't very far from Bannon. And the reason she is going there, instead of staying home and going to the U or else to theater school, is because it has a super drama department. They've got a new director with a name that sounds something like Ustinoff, and Grandda says he's tops."

She could tell Bruce wasn't listening. Maybe he got tired of hearing so much about her family. She said, "I forgot to ask you. Did Aunt Vinia come to the relations' dinner on Christmas Day? And did Jake ever paste the St. Jude picture over the stair window?"

"What? Oh, no, Aunt Vinia didn't come. I forgot what excuse she gave, but I figure she was afraid Mom would start the old routine of how much better off she'd be in a nursing home. What'd you say about Jake?"

"The picture? Did he paste it over the window for her?"

"I don't think he's got around to it yet."

They were approaching the Purple Cow drive-in on the Boulevard. She expected him to ask, "Hungry?" the way he always did just to hear her say, "Yeh, starvelous," and then he would say, "That's marvelous. There's nothing I like better than feeding the starvelous." Instead he drove past the Purple Cow and headed for the park.

Almost of its own volition, the car came to a stop in front of the duck pond. "Had I but known," Stacy said, "I could have brought the ducks the leftover piece of fruitcake that Claire had. You don't suppose they would have minded citron in it, do you?"

He didn't answer. They sat in silence a moment or two.

"I have news for you, Stacy," he said abruptly. "This car is mine now. I mean all mine. Mom is getting a smaller one—not quite a mini—but one she can handle easier. She still has to save that right arm. I guess there's some nerve damage or something." He repeated, "Mom is getting a smaller one that's easier to park. So she gave me this one."

"Oh." She wished it had been the other way around. She wished that his mother had kept this one, so pervaded by the lingering scent of her perfume, which Stacy thought was Fauberge, and that Bruce would be driving his own unscented one.

Bruce moved restively behind the wheel. He was whacking one gloved fist into the palm of the other. "And I've got some more news. I'm going out for basketball. The coach wants me to try out for the freshman team."

"Oh, wonderful. You'll be their crack basket thrower."

"That's what they need. That's what the coach said. He's new this year." He was talking in the stiff choppy sentences the way he always did when he was uneasy about something. "Mom had him over to dinner. He said he saw me play when I was at Adams High. He's in quite a fever about putting out a winning team. Says the sports world pays more attention to the freshman team than anyone realizes." He gave a forced laugh. "He's got the rep of being a regular Simon Legree. But as he says, you have to work the tail off guys if you want to get anywhere."

She put in an agreeing "You sure do."

"He's weak on basket throwers, he says. And you know, Stacy, how a lot of games are won or lost by making foul throws. I'm a bit rusty. But it won't take long to get the old throwing arm back. I'll practice with the fellows. Then I'll stay on and shoot baskets to better my average." He paused and then continued, "Coach has already lined up a lot of practice games.

Every team he can get them with—in Denver and out. Because, as he says, it's in a game that a team's weaknesses really show up."

Another pause while he looked not at Stacy but at the squawking ducks, greedily gobbling up the bread other people had tossed into the water. "That's why Mom turned this car over to me. Because I'll have a darn tight schedule."

Her lips formed a soundless O. She was puzzled, not by what he was telling her, but by his fidgety uneasiness. There was something she couldn't quite put her finger on. "Are you trying to break it to me that you won't be able to pick me up after school, Bruce, except maybe once in awhile? You don't have to hem and haw about that." She thought back to his last year at Adams High and to his saying "I might be a little late tomorrow" or "Don't look for me on Wednesday, but there'll be just a short workout the following day." She added, "It's all right—I know how it is."

He was still fiddling with his gloved hands. This time he spread his fingers into V's, and he shoved the V's on one hand back and forth with the other as though he were trying to make the new leather gloves fit better between his fingers.

"I won't be able to make it *any* afternoons. And Saturdays—Well, as I said, the coach has practice games scheduled."

Again her lips formed an O as she too stared out at the lake. But now he did turn and look at her. He pulled off his gloves and caught her hand, and his words came in an excited rush. "But wait till I tell you.

I have to take a language this semester. I'm signing up for Spanish. Everyone says it's easier than French or German. Besides, Jake has conversational Spanish records. He got them so's to soak up the language before he hitchhiked to Mexico last summer. I can tell the folks I have to listen to them. So we can get together on Sunday. We can pull that Jake deal again."

She said slowly, "I don't like it. It was sort of fun—I mean at first I thought it was fun—to slip something over on your folks. But it's sneaky."

He ignored that and went on swiftly, "Jake spends a lot of time now at the Student Union. I guess you've heard that it's being all done over and enlarged. The art students—the good ones—are painting murals on the walls. Jake's doing one—maybe two. His place would be a lot more private than Downey's where people are always stopping to talk to us. I can load the car up with Cokes and take them over there. Jake's got a stereo and some swell records."

Her puzzled eyes rested on him. She was getting closer to being able to put her mind's finger on that elusive something that puzzled her. "You mean that no one would see us together at Jake's, but that if we sat in the booth at Downey's, someone who knew your mother or father might see us and tell them we were there together."

He almost shouted, "What I do on Sundays is my own business."

She pulled her hand out of his and moved over to her side of the seat. She buttoned up the green St. Jude blazer—even the top button at the throat—as though some of the misty chill outside had seeped into her.

"All right, all right," Bruce said. "If your going through the Jake routine sticks in your craw, you don't have to do it. Did I tell you that Jake's got a pretty beat-up cabin in the foothills that he's trying to fix up? I've gone up with him some Sundays to help"—again he gave that nervous excited laugh—"He may be a good painter, but he's sure a dodo about putting glass in windows or hinges on doors. I'm a lot better at those things than he is. And it's not far—just an hour's drive."

She stiffened slightly, guessing what was coming next.

"It's swell up there, Stacy. You'd love it. I was thinking what fun we could have, tramping around and feeding the chipmunks." She could hear the eager pleading excitement building up in him. "The last time I was up there with Jake, I worked on the chimney, so the fireplace oughtn't to smoke now. We can cook steak on it. Or else I can pick up some of those boxes of chicken and French fries. We can even have slaw for vitamins. I've been thinking about it all day."

"And thinking too about how safe it would be," she put in. "Thinking about how your folks wouldn't know you were with me. Take me home, Bruce."

With a grunt of disgust and fury, he started the motor and jerkily backed the car around. They drove home in stony silence except for her "Let me out at our gate." (Not under our own weeping willow, she meant.)

He stopped with a jerk at the side of her house. "Look, Stacy," he pleaded, "You know I've always been crazy about sports. Lord, how I envied the fellows playing football last fall when I saw them suited up and trotting out on the field, and I couldn't go out for it because Mom had to have me get her places and bring her back."

Someone—Stacy couldn't remember whether it was Claire or Ben's Jeanie—had said, "I never saw a collarbone take as long to heal as Mrs. Seerie's." But she did remember that it was Mother who had added, "She uses her broken collarbone to keep Bruce on a tight tether."

Bruce talked on. "Honest, Stacy, you'll never know how I've been itching to get my hands on a ball again. You know how there's nothing as great as hearing that sound of the ball slipping through the basket."

"Yes, I know. I'm glad you're playing."

"And you know how a guy who goofs off on his subjects can't stay on the team. It'll take me two or three hours every night to keep my marks up. And in training you have to hit the sack at ten every night. That's what the coach said. No tom-catting around at night."

Again she spoke slowly, gropingly, "I guess that Poison Ivy woman didn't waste any time telling your folks she saw us at Schmitty's. Did your mother—or maybe your dad—go to the coach and invite him to dinner? Maybe they told him you needed a tighter tether." She shoved open the door of the car and got out.

He tumbled out his side of the car, rounded the hood, and caught her arm. "I thought you'd understand." Anger gave his voice a higher pitch.

"I understand all right. I've seen enough squeeze plays on the field to know one when I see it."

He laughed in sudden exultance, and gave her arm a shake. "Don't think I don't know a squeeze play myself. I'm not that dumb. Let's say, I saw them closing in on me, but I saw a hole through which to get free. Let's say, I was chuckling to myself, thinking of how we could still be together on Sunday and still keep everybody happy."

"Let's say, I think you're more low-down and scurvy than I thought. Even people who take bribes are supposed to do whatever they're bribed to do." She wrenched away from him and started for the gate. The exultation and color had drained from his face, leaving it slack and pale.

She got through the gate, but again he clutched her arm and held onto it across the closed gate. "I don't see why you're so mad about my wanting us to be together on Sundays either at Jake's or at his cabin."

"I'm not mad." She only wished she were. Where was her good old Irish temper? Rage would be better than this feeling of hopeless weariness. Her voice was flat. "Did you have to sign an agreement that you wouldn't see me before your mother turned over her nice, shiny, scented car to you?"

"That's the shanty Irish in you," he hurled out. "Saying the hatefulest thing you can think of. Look, I told you I was sorry I couldn't pick you up after school."

"Don't worry about that. I can always get a ride home in Obie's hearse. Obie goes out for sports too, but he works extra at a supermarket, and he bought the hearse with his own money. So there're no strings attached to it. He can take anyone he wants in it. And you can tell your mother she needn't worry either. Because I'll never put foot in that car again—never."

"You don't mean that. It's my car now," he yelled as though she were ten feet away from him instead of a mere foot with only a gate between.

"*Your car!* It's the carrot held in front of the donkey."

"And I'm the donkey, I suppose."

"You're the donkey," she agreed in a lackluster voice. "You're the donkey following the carrot, and the car is the carrot dangling in front of your nose so you'll follow along wherever they want you to go." She looked beyond him and said musingly, "When I first knew you, I thought you were the strong rugged type. I thought you were more of a man than any boy I knew. I always felt so protected when I was with you. Do you remember telling me that you wanted to protect me from all turmoil? But the joke of that is that once before when I needed you, I couldn't get to you. Because *they* were protecting you from me. I remember how furious I was at Jeanie Kincaid when she told me you were parent-ridden. I hated Mom for saying you were under your mother's thumb. I—I just couldn't believe it was true."

"For godsake, goon. I live with them. They're paying my way through school. What do you want me to do? Kick them in the teeth? And now you're sore because Mom has turned over the car to me. What do you want me to do? Hoof it three miles home after basketball practice when I'm already limp as a rag? Yeh, and mooch rides the best way I can when we have out-of-town games. I have to have a car." He was shouting again.

She knew that he was beating around the bush, that the numb lump inside of her was because he hadn't had the guts to stand up and say, "I'll give everything I've got to basketball, but I still want to see Stacy whenever I can crowd it in." So what was the use of arguing?

A pleading note crept back into his voice. "Ah, Stacy, I never thought you'd be like this. You don't mean that you won't *ever* date me again?"

"I mean," she said tiredly, "that I've had all I can take of a mama and papa's boy that has to sneak around and lie to see me. Was it part of all the plans you've made to have me hunch down on the floor of the car so no one would see me until we got out of town?"

She wrenched away from him. He might have held on to her if he had clutched her with his bare hand, but he had on his new gloves, with the leather that was still a little stiff in spite of all his fiddling and thumping, and her arm slipped out of his grasp.

She didn't look back as she walked into the house. She heard without feeling, for she was still wrapped in a blanket of numbness, the well-known whir of the motor starting in the copper-brown car and its well-adjusted purr as Bruce drove off in it down the street.

5 ～

IT WAS strange that a girl who had just been squeezed out of a boy's life could walk into the house without feeling even a twinge of pain. It was as if she had suddenly become an automaton. Wrapped in the frozen numbness, she moved and reacted mechanically.

When her mother held up for her inspection what had been a ruffled old-fashioned white blouse that she had dyed orchid to wear with a purple velvet skirt at Guido's Gay Nineties, Stacy was able to voice her admiration. She could answer her mother's "But look at these awful purple hands. What do you suppose will whiten them up for tonight?" with "Maybe that cleanser we use on the sink would help."

She could even sit and drink tea—though the tea had a brackish flavor—with only an odd feeling of unreality, a feeling that the boy to whom she had said, "I'll never put foot in that car again," was not the same boy who had said to her on December twenty-third, "Some day we'll be married." She couldn't possibly have said

"You're the donkey following the carrot" to the Bruce she had looked up to and all but idolized.

At school the next day she continued to go through the motions. At noontime she listened to Liesel's usual prattle about how smooth the course of true love was running between her and Big Sully. (It would as long as it was kept secret from Papa Muehler.) And Stacy said nothing about the course of her own true love, which had hit an insurmountable snag.

She barely listened when Claire interrupted Liesel's chatter to tell them, "Sister Therese has a momentous project afoot for our whole senior class. Oh, my, yes! She talked it over with St. Jude. He's given his approval, so now she's wholly dedicated to it. And we might as well get ready to be—or pretend to be—dedicated too."

"Did she tell you what it was?" Liesel asked curiously.

"She had to let it out a little because she wanted me to round up some books for her." (Claire worked in her free time in the library to pay for her tuition.) "But Sister Therese will drop the bombshell herself when the time comes."

Claire refused to say more in spite of Liesel's pleading, but Stacy wasn't even interested enough to pry further.

That afternoon she rode home in Obie's hearse, and walked into the house to find it in a great to-do of Christmas tree dismantling.

"It's Twelfth Night," Jill announced importantly. "So when we get all the trimming off, we're going to chop up the tree and burn it. The angel that Bruce mended is still mended."

Good for the angel!

Stacy ran the vacuum, giving her whole mind to certain little fine threads of tinsel that clung tightly to the old rug.

It wasn't until Thursday that the numbness gave way to a throbbing ache. Claire, all unwittingly, wanting to be helpful, started it. Liesel was at home with one of her frequent colds, so that only the two of them sat together in their corner of the lunchroom.

In the privacy provided by the clatter of dishes and babel of voices, Claire leaned across the table to ask abruptly, "When's the last time you saw Bruce?"

"Monday."

"Haven't you heard from him since?"

"No, I have not heard from him since" was Stacy's clipped reply.

Claire looked at her with stricken concern, then burst out, "Then it's true what that old blabbermouth next door said."

Stacy gave a mirthless laugh. "I don't know what she said. But if she said his folks worked a squeeze play to keep Bruce from seeing Stacy Belford, she's right. I'm sure her telling them about seeing us dancing at Schmitty's threw the fear of God in them and—"

"That wasn't all that threw the fear of God in them. Bruce's mother heard about Aunt Vinia giving you her turquoise beads."

"I didn't think Aunt Vinia would tell her."

"She didn't. Some girl did. It was the one Mama

Seerie thinks would be more suitable for Bruce, because her folks have moved here and her father is a big-shot contractor—"

"Joyce!" Stacy breathed. "Joyce Black-something. I told her that Bruce's Aunt Vinia gave me the beads."

"Where in the world did you see Joyce to tell her?"

"She was at that frat party in a white dress, and she—"

"The frat party where you didn't get enough to eat?"

"Where I didn't get *anything* to eat but a sliver of cheese. And that's where a girl who brought peanuts said that Joyce had let them all think she was Bruce's date that night."

Claire's eyes took on the same alert and unblinking concentration they did in Math when she watched the teacher propound a theorem in geometry. "I can see Mama S.'s fine Italian hand in that too. Because why would Joyce pass around the word that she was to be Bruce's date if she didn't think so herself? Because—I'll just bet my barbed wire!—Bruce's mother told her that Bruce would be there as soon as he took a present out to Aunt Vinia. Yes, and I'll bet she even said something to Bruce about his meeting Joyce there. And Bruce probably kept his mouth shut to his mother about his taking you."

"More than probably," Stacy agreed with another dry laugh. "Old peace-at-any-price Bruce." And that was when the throbbing hurt started. *Why couldn't Bruce have said, "That's fine with me if Joyce goes, but I'm taking Stacy."?*

Claire went on, "You know why the Senior Seeries

want everything real cozy between them and the Black-something family—it's Black*well*, I just remembered. Not that you'd get the real lowdown from old boot-licking Englemann. But Blackwell is putting up all those town houses for the elite out by Delmar Dam, and a big outfit like that always needs a lawyer. And who would be sharper at keeping them within legal limits than Papa Seerie, attorney at law?"

"The Seeries had the Black-whatever-it-ises over to Christmas Eve dinner." This time Stacy could only manage a down-twisted smile. "I hope Mr. Seerie didn't hurt his chances when he was so late getting there. Bruce told me about it."

"Oh, yes, we heard about that 'unfortunate affair' too. Old Seerie must have had a lot of Christmas cheer in him to play Good Samaritan to that poor gal who broke her leg at the office party."

"She didn't break her leg. She strained a legament."

"*Li*gament. And don't claim that if it's in the leg it ought to be legament, because ligaments are also scattered around in other places."

Bruce had corrected her pronunciation too. The lump of pain gave another twinge. But just as one must probe with the tongue that hurting spot where a tooth has been pulled, Stacy found herself asking, "And did Poison Ivy tell you that the Seeries are now licking their chops because they pulled Bruce out of my clutches?"

"Come now. Let's not be crass," Claire said in her mimicking voice. "It's simply that parents have the best interests of their children at heart. Too many young people have gotten carried away and jeopardized their future, and Bruce's parents believe he must give his whole attention right now to schoolwork and sports. That's the sanctimonious tack the Ivy woman took. I'm just reading between the lines about the Seeries buddying up to the Blackwells, and their shoving Bruce at Joyce as part of the buddying-up. Did you and Bruce have an honest-to-God battle?"

Stacy poured out the whole story to Claire's sympathetic head shakings and tch, tch, tchs. "I don't know why I didn't get mad. Not even when I told him he was low-down and scurvy, and that I'd had all I wanted of a mama's boy." She could still see the deflated look on Bruce's drained face. "You can tell that to your Poison Ivy the next time she comes by to gloat."

"It isn't gloating—not exactly. It's just that she knows what good friends you and I are, and so she has to harp on the Seeries and the-best-interests-of-their-son angle. She even admitted how attractive and charming you looked that night in December, and how beautifully you sang."

"Fancy that."

"And I told her you could get any boy you wanted, and that you certainly wouldn't be the sort to sit at home, grieving your heart out for Bruce Seerie."

"You're darn right I won't. I didn't when we broke up before, or when his folks sent him back to Lincoln to separate us."

But then, of course, Bruce had returned last fall, and that strong magnetic force between them had sent them winging into each other's arms. That indescribable pull—it had always brought them together again after even their bitterest fights.

Claire asked as they wadded up the paper bags, containing orange skins and bread crusts, "Are you sure, hon, it's the fight to end all fights? I mean, if Bruce drove up to St. Jude's, are you sure you wouldn't climb into that nice shiny copper-colored car again?"

"I'll never set foot in that perfumed car again. That, I'm sure of. And Bruce won't ask me. Not after what I said. I'm sure of that too."

But there was something she couldn't explain to Claire. She couldn't even explain it to herself clearly. Had she just imagined a Bruce Seerie who was capable of making decisions for himself and of sheltering a girl from all turmoil? That was the Bruce she had lost her heart to. The fight to end all fights had been not with him, but with the parent-dominated, the peace-at-any-price, one. And maybe this strange unfinished feeling was the hope that the first Bruce would be drawn back to her. It was because of this hope that her eyes still lifted each afternoon when she pushed through St. Jude's heavy doors, that her heart still set up a clamoring rat-a-tat-tat each time the doorbell or phone rang in the house on Hubbell Street.

She and Claire joined the queue at the trash can on the way out of the lunchroom. Claire moved closer to ask in a low mutter, "Hey, how about the green necklace Aunt Vinia gave you? Are you going to keep it?"

"I wish now she hadn't given it to me. Mom says turquoises are worth a lot more today than when Aunt

Vinia first got it. But . . . I don't . . . know. I keep wondering about it."

"Maybe you could write Emily Post and ask her if a girl should return a necklace to a grandaunt when she has broken off with the grandnephew because he has turned out very *un*grand."

On Sunday, Stacy stood again at the side of the altar with the other musicians holding their guitars. The poinsettias had given way to pink and white carnations, but again the center aisle was filled with communicants—the same young fathers and mothers carrying babies that couldn't be left in the pew, the same arthritic woman in the wheelchair, the same children with their Christmas parkas and boots looking a bit scuffed by now.

Again Stacy chorded her guitar while the more professional strummed out the melody. Again the four on the altar sang with the congregation: "*O Lord, cum ba ya.*"

Stacy waited for that swelling of peace and exaltation and love. Nothing happened. The numb weight under her ribs stayed right there. She had no feeling of the hem of a garment brushing her—or even of its coming near.

6 ❧

*J*ANUARY, the month of long nights. And snowy days. Snow to be waded through. Snow that a bright sun turned to slush that found every leak in last year's boots. Slush that a bitter wind froze into lumpy ice to make walking or driving precarious. And more snow. The early-morning rasp of snow shovels, and Ben carping at Matt and Brian for the slapdash way they cleaned the walks.

"Why can't *she* do any shoveling?" Matt would grumble back.

The *she*, of course, was Jill who on previous winters had huffed and puffed, shoveled and scraped along with her brothers. But now Jill was a junior miss, and all too conscious of the boys in her class, especially of Itsy Sullivan.

"Stacy, you'd never guess what Cathie Ott did today. She wore lipstick to school. And do you know what she told Sister? She said it was salve, and she said her mother made her put it on because her lips were chapped. She'd do anything to make Itsy notice her.

She's still mad because he gave me that ring he won in the gumball machine at Downey's Drug."

The eternal triangle. Only it was a minx in a mink jacket who formed one side of Stacy's.

January, the month of edgy tempers. When the smell of the white mice in their cage in Matt's and Brian's room permeated the whole upstairs, Mother exploded at her two younger sons. "Either you clean that cage, or both cage and mice get dumped into the ashcan."

Stacy's own mood toward the littles varied from tenderness to temper outbursts to tears.

Brian, the youngest of the Belfords, was naturally a grave and gentle little boy although he tried to imitate Matt's tough façade. He had already lost the Christmas mittens Liz had knitted him. On a below-zero afternoon when he came home from school, Stacy rubbed his stiff and purplish hands to warmness. "Ah, honey love, I've got a pair of warm gloves you can wear."

But when Matt sneered, "Gloves, *girls'* gloves," she turned on him with such wrath that he involuntarily dodged her clenched fist. "Shut up, you poisonous brat," she shouted. "A lot you care if his hands freeze and drop off. I don't see you lending him your *boys'* mittens—or even one of them."

It wasn't until an evening in late January, on a Friday which was the night Mother had off from Guido's supper club, that she and Stacy got around to gathering up the clumps of Christmas cards from piano, bookshelves, and mantel. They carried them out to the dinette table to sort, to jot down address changes, and to read over the messages on them.

Mother was the kind of person who muttered her thoughts aloud as she worked. She reread the note from Grandfather Belford who ever since a bout with pneumonia several years ago always spent the winter in the warmer climate of Phoenix. "Imagine that sweet old fellow all alone on Christmas. It just isn't right. Not that it would bother your fine Aunt Eustace."

On Mother's side of the family there were more relatives than anyone could count. All those O'Byrnes and Callahans and "loose connections." But on the Belford side, they could be counted on your two thumbs: Grandfather Belford and the unmarried Aunt Eustace.

Mother sometimes quoted, "God gives us our relations, but thank God we can pick our friends." To this, she now added with unwonted spleen, "But God doesn't give us our in-laws, and we can't pick them either." She didn't mean the kindly, scholarly Grandfather Belford but her husband's sister, Eustace. "That stuck-up selfish flibbertigibbet," she ground out under her breath.

Stacy paid little heed. She was rereading a card from a boy named Pete. He was the guitar player who had taught her the chords she strummed at the folk Mass and who had gone back to Kansas to stay with his parents for Christmas. "Pete sounds as if he will be staying on at home," she said. "He's playing with a group back there—looks like the Cornhuskers. I can hardly read his writing."

"We'll all miss Pete dropping in," Mother murmured. "He was always sweet—and always hungry."

Stacy would miss him too. Nice easy-going Pete with

his lopsided grin who thought the world was filled with beautiful people. Never an exchange of hateful words with him. Never any hammering of the heart either.

Mother said very casually, for of course she had noticed that it was Obie's hearse that stopped to let Stacy off after school, "Aren't you seeing Bruce anymore?"

Stacy fairly spat out the words. "No. I am not seeing Bruce anymore. And, no, I don't expect to. So go ahead with all your I-told-you-so's. Go ahead and sing hallelujah!"

Ordinarily such an outburst would have drawn a swift response from Mother. Stacy somehow wished it had. Mother only looked at her and then lowered her eyes, so like Stacy's own blue ones, full now of aching pity to the heavy oversize envelope in front of her.

Absently she pulled out the large shiny card and tossed the envelope on the table. Stacy knew from the airmail stamps and stickers that it was from Aunt Eustace. The address contained no street number or street, just Seven Elms, Godalming, Surrey, England."

Mother gave vent to her feelings about the card she held: "Her and her natter about wassail parties, and hunting the Yule log. Seven Elms, Godalming. God almighty! You'd think she'd want to spend Christmas with her father instead of with those horsey cousins over there. She's ten years older than I am, and she thinks she's still eighteen."

Stacy couldn't trust her voice to answer. The card sorting went on. Mother said suddenly, "Stacy, did I ever tell you about the first time I went with your father to visit Grandfather Belford and Aunt Eustace? Before your father and I were married?"

Feeling uncomfortable pangs of guilt for having lashed out at her, Stacy pretended an interest she didn't feel. "No, I don't think so."

"God help us, I can still cringe when I think of it."

"Why?"

"Why because I was such a small-town gawk and didn't have sense enough to know it. I thought I was a knockout. I thought the ensemble I'd bought at the Elite Shoppe in Bannon was the last word—a Kelly-green dress with an imitation fox jacket. And my friends had given me a going-away present—a necklace and earring set of brassy gold with green stones set like marbles—and a bracelet too—the clanky kind. All Bannon thought I was ravishing in them." She shuddered in rueful memory. "And thus decked out, I went with Matthew to tea at the Belford mansion to meet his father and his sister Eustace."

"Hadn't you met either of them before?"

"No, not *met*. Oh, of course, I'd seen Chancellor Belford at the university, and I'd heard him give a lecture on Renaissance lyrics. And I'd seen pictures and write-ups galore of Eustace Belford in the society columns. You see, I'd only known your father a month when we decided to get married."

Stacy knew about that whirlwind romance which, so Jeanie Kincaid's mother said, had been the talk of the campus. How Rose O'Byrne with her dream of being a concert pianist had come from Bannon to enroll at the university, how that first week she had gone to the library to get a book on the various movements of the sonata, and how a young man named Matthew Belford, doing research for his master's had looked up and seen her.

Mother said now, "I can remember every detail of that afternoon as plain as if it was yesterday. Matthew ushering me through those heavy iron gates, and up the curved walk past the lily pond. And the statue of the deer with the wolf trying to bring it down. . . ."

Stacy put in, "Remember how Brian used to worry about that statue? And how every time any of us went there and came back, he'd ask, 'Did the wolf get the deer yet?'"

Mother laughed. "Not yet, it hasn't." She reminisced on. "And the house. I'd heard it called the Belford mansion, but it seemed like a palace to me, compared to the dumpy little frame houses in Bannon."

"Were they nice to you—Grandfather and Aunt Eustace?"

"Grandfather was a love. I remember the feeling of his warm thin hands taking hold of mine. And I can still remember exactly what he said: 'So you're Rose. I don't wonder that Matthew has a hard time putting his mind on his thesis. You're as beautiful as he said, and all heart besides.' And he kissed me"—Mother's voice thickened—"and he said he was happy to have me for a daughter . . ."

"Don't cry, for gosh sakes. What did Aunt Eustace say?"

Mother's choky voice turned harsh. "Not that she

was happy to have me for a sister, you can just bet. She wasn't there at first. She came in later from a Junior League tea or meeting. She slid out of a darkish brown fur coat. She had on a sort of beige wool dress. *Her* earrings were tiny pearls. I didn't realize then that her coat was sable, and her dress a Paris original. And me in my Elite Shoppe ensemble! I only know that the moment she came into the room and turned her eyes on me, I knew that my clothes and my laugh were too loud, and I felt all feet and low-Irish."

"Did she say anything?"

"She didn't need to. Her looks said it for her." Mother pushed herself up from the table and paced to the window and back again. "I was such a green lout of a thing, Stacy. The housekeeper served us tea. I was so awed by the silver tea service and those delicate china cups, thin as eggshells—"

"I know," Stacy said out of her own experience of having tea at the Belford mansion. "And lemon slices with cloves stuck in them, and sandwiches about as big as dominoes."

Mother nodded with a shaky laugh. "Oh, yes, a far cry from our tea in Bannon where we all sat around the kitchen table and had to weaken the strong brew with milk and sugar. And our thick slices of Irish bread with blackberry jam. Matthew told the housekeeper that I took milk in my tea, and she brought some. But I'd already put a lemon slice in it, and I didn't know whether to take it out or leave it in. I was so nervous that I kept gulping down the sandwiches and *petits fours*."

(71)

She got up again and paced to the window and looked out at the dark snowy scene outside. "And there sat Miss Eustace, sipping her tea and talking about her Junior League meeting, and how they were planning to bring Iturbi to Denver. Oh, yes, she had heard him play Tschaikovsky's First Piano Concerto in B-flat in New York. Heavens above, Stacy," she demanded tautly, "what do you suppose—after her throwing Iturbi and Tschaikovsky at me—made me yammer, yammer, yammer on? Wouldn't you have thought I'd have had wits enough to keep my mouth shut?"

"What did you yammer, yammer, yammer about?"

"About *my* playing, if you please. About my only having taken piano lessons for six months, and how I could play anything from "Roll out the Barrel" to Brahms' "Lullaby." How I always played for all the weddings and funerals in Bannon and all around the country. And how my father had been with the Abbey Players in Dublin. Old brag-and-blow me. I knew I was talking too much—but I couldn't stop. And *her* listening to it all with a God-have-mercy look on her face." Mother paused with a tortured look on her face. "That was the beginning," she said. "All these years she's had that same look-down-her-nose attitude—that I was an ignorant little upstart who didn't belong with the Belfords, that I had somehow hooked poor Matthew. . . ."

"Didn't Father and Grandfather Belford know how she always high-hatted you?"

"Yes, they did. But Matthew never took Eustace and her airs and graces seriously. He couldn't understand why it should rankle me so." There was another, longer pause, and then Mother said, "I've often thought of how *hellish* life would have been if Matthew hadn't seen through her—or if he had been under his sister's thumb."

Stacy had listened with complete empathy to it all. But at that last sentence, she stiffened. So there was hidden meaning to this recital. Her lips thinned. "I take it there's a moral to all this sad tale."

Once again Mother did not flare up. She only said slowly, "The moral of this sad tale is that it would have been far sadder if Matthew hadn't stood with me against her. Oh, my dear own, you and I are alike. You could never draw a happy breath either if someone treated you like scum."

Stacy dropped the sheaf of Christmas cards she was holding with such force that they scattered over the table and onto the floor. "All right, all right," she screamed. "I told you Bruce and I are all washed up, didn't I? So stop rubbing it in about his folks treating me like scum."

Mother let that outburst go by unnoticed also. "I'd like you to realize that it's better for you to take the hurt now—and have it over with," she said, and began to pick up the cards strewn on the floor.

Stacy hurled herself off the dinette bench, muttering that she had to wash a blouse for tomorrow. She sudsed and swished it out in the washbowl upstairs with tears blinding her eyes, so that she washed one cuff twice and the other not at all.

It's like getting a tooth pulled, she kept telling herself. *It hurts for awhile, and then you just feel the vacant place where the tooth used to be.*

(73)

7 ∿

 $F_{EBRUARY}$ was better. As though to make amends for January's vicious storms, the second month of the year came in with sunny skies and soft winds.

Stacy's inner climate was less tempestuous too. The hurt was easing. But there was still the gap, still the unfinished feeling. Sometimes she berated herself bitterly, *Weren't you the dope ever to think he was the strong rugged type!* But again, lying in bed beside the sleeping Jill, she would think longingly, *If I could just see him* once *more. If I could just be sure he's all mama's boy. Then I could make myself forget. Then I could go on from there.*

On the first Monday in February Sister Therese assembled the seventy-eight members of St. Jude's graduating class in the auditorium, and "dumped Bernadette in their laps" as the seniors put it. Her eyes aglow and rapt, she announced, "I have called you together to talk over your senior play. I have given much thought and prayer to it."

Sister Therese taught Lit and Drama. She was no newcomer to the theater. She had majored in it at college. She had played in the little theater before she donned the robes of a teaching nun. In past years and under her tutelage, the St. Jude senior classes had put on creditable productions of *Carousel* and *Romeo and Juliet*. For one so fragile and devout, she was an indefatigable worker.

She stood before them that Monday morning, slender and taut with suppressed eagerness. She led into her talk by telling them that their graduating class was closer and dearer to her than any she had ever taught. "And that's why I'd like our senior play this year to be something—something memorable and long-lasting—"

Claire nudged Stacy. "Here comes the bombshell," she whispered. "Here comes Bernadette."

The bombshell and Bernadette came. Sister Therese held up a thickish book. "This is *The Song of Bernadette* that Franz Werfel was inspired to write about the simple and sickly little French peasant girl who saw the vision of Our Lady in a messy rubbish-filled cave. And, as you know, because of her vision, Lourdes is now a mecca to which the afflicted of the world journey. The pile of crutches and wheelchairs testify to the miracles that happen there.

One of the boys muttered aloud, "Be a good place for the football team to go for crutches." And a girl's stunned voice asked, "You mean there's a play about it?"

Sister Therese shook her head and, in her intense eagerness, drew a few steps nearer to her audience. "No,

I mean that we—you seniors and I—will write our own two-act play from the book and put it on ourselves."

Her words tumbled out. Couldn't they see how much more meaningful and more rewarding this would be than merely buying copies of a play and following the words and directions of someone else?

"Ah, Sister," Obie pleaded, "can't we have a musical, so Stacy can sing her way through it? We've got a neat ballet dancer too. And I'll be the funny man."

Again Sister Therese shook her head. She had thought of their doing a musical. She had thought of a comedy with lots of laughs. But it seemed to her that right now the world needed something more than high jinks or guffaws. It needed to be reminded of miracles and simple faith.

The seniors looked helplessly at each other and squirmed. But they stifled their groans. It wasn't only that they all loved the little sister because of her own loving devotion to them, but that they felt a certain protectiveness toward her. Last fall when she had been delegated to give the girls a lecture on love, courtship, and marriage, the girls had listened with grave attention, and with never a nudge or a wink at each other, although every one of her listeners knew far more about the subject than the earnest, gentle, doe-eyed nun. And last fall when a new pupil had made an audible wisecrack at something Sister Therese said, Obie had turned gimlet eyes upon him. "Your teeth might look better halfway down your throat," he had snarled.

The meeting ended with Sister Therese and Claire handing out all the copies of *The Song of Bernadette* they had been able to find. Each recipient accepted the book with what Stacy's mother called a God-give-me-strength look. "As you read it, make copious notes," Sister told them. "And keep in mind which incidents would have the most dramatic impact in our play." When the readers finished, they were to pass the books on to those still needing a copy, she added. "I can't wait until you've all read it," she finished with almost girlish delight, "and then we'll discuss together all our findings and insights."

"She must think we're geniuses," Stacy muttered to Claire.

"She does—and saints besides. Wait for me while I run down to the library and back."

Stacy waited outside the auditorium door. Some of the students who passed her seemed in too much of a state of shock to say a word. Only Liesel seemed happy. "Maybe Papa will let me take a part in this be-cause it's uplifting," she said.

Stacy opened the book she had been allotted, and flicked through the pages. Oh, dear! Fine print, a jum-ble of unpronounceable French names, and very little dialogue.

Sister Therese was the last to come out the door. She slid an arm around Stacy. "I had to say a little prayer of thanksgiving because my hare-brained project—that's what Sister Cabrina calls it—was so well re-ceived."

"Sister, were you always so good?"

The nun laughed self-disparagingly. "Oh, child, child, don't ever say that. Being good takes so much working at. It's going forward one step, and then falling back two. It always comforts me to read the lives of the saints, because even they—even though they had their brief epiphanies—"

"What's that?"

"It's a lifting up and opening up of the heart. A sort of feeling of revelation and of at-oneness with God. But, alas, it's very short-lived."

If that brief lifting up and opening up of her heart on Christmas morning could be called an epiphany, it was certainly short-lived.

"But all the saints confess to constant irritations in daily living. Strange, isn't it, Stacy, that we're able to rise to life's crushing catastrophes or tragedies? Somehow, they seem to bring out the nobility in us. But it's the little things, the daily pinpricks, that try the soul beyond words."

Oh, yes, those constant pinpricks that a happier Stacy had never noticed. Jill's constant rehashing of the seventh-grade triangle between Itsy Sullivan, Cathie Ott, and herself. Ben's grim insistence that Stacy make the school lunches the night before. Liesel's pleased prattle all through lunchtime about Big Sully. And even Katie Rose writing so ecstatically about her drama class under the teacher with a name something like Ustinoff.

"Do you have pinpricks to try your soul, Sister? I can't imagine it."

Little Sister Therese, who wasn't as tall as Stacy and weighed even less than her 110 pounds, looked up and down the hall to see if anyone was within earshot. "If you'll promise never to breathe it, Stacy, I'll tell you what does try my soul—snapshots. Especially those colored ones you have to look at through a whatever-you-call it that you hold up to the light. One of the sisters here is always clutching my arm with a stack of them of her nieces and nephews saying their prayers, running through the hose, blowing out birthday candles. I have to ask God to forgive me, because sometimes when I see her bearing down on me, I put my glasses in my pocket and pretend I left them in chapel with my missal."

Stacy laughed joyfully. "I love you more than ever, Sister."

Partly because of Sister Therese's enthusiasm, partly because she wanted something to focus her whole mind on, Stacy attacked the Bernadette book with fervor. The fervor lasted for two evenings of reading.

The next noontime she said to Claire, who had already read the book through, "It wasn't too bad reading about Bernadette's drunken father. Or her mother trying to scrounge up enough food for them—golly, that damp old dump they lived in—and Bernadette's asthma—"

"Nobody was nice to her either," Liesel put in. "Her teacher called her stupid, and her sister was such a smart aleck."

"How far did you get in the book, Stacy?" Claire asked.

"I got through her going with the girls to pick up wood. And her seeing the Lady, as she called her, standing in that filthy, smelly cave. But then I bogged down with all the people and all the politics and squabbling."

"Did you get as far as the village priest thinking she was lying? And all but picking her up by the scruff of the neck and tossing her out?"

Stacy shook her head. "All those French names—I didn't know who were the good guys and who were the villains."

"Well, I admit it was quite a hassle. Some thought it was all a hoax, and some were amazed at the cures. But everyone—all the town officials and the politicians and businessmen—wanted to get in on the act because each one saw ways of making money out of it. And there was poor little Bernadette right in the middle, getting it from all sides."

Liesel spoke again. "She went and became a nun. I knew that without reading the book."

"But not until years later," Claire the authority said. "I guess it was the one way to find a little peace."

"I think I'll be a nun," Stacy said.

"Hah!" Claire snorted. "I think I'll be Miss America."

On one of the balmy springlike days, Stacy stopped at Pearl's Bakery on the Boulevard on her way home from school. She pushed through the door, juggling schoolbooks, a very large bag of sandwich bread, and a slightly smaller one of cupcakes. The smell of the chocolate icing on the cupcakes was too tantalizing to resist, and she reached into the bag for one.

She had finished it and was licking the icing off her fingers when a voice hailed, "Well, if it isn't little Stacy with the green eyes, licking her sticky paws."

She looked up to meet the rakish grin of Bruce's friend Jake. "You can have a cupcake too," she offered.

He took one promptly, and demolished it in two bites. In the bright sun he looked even more gaunt and shabby than he had looked that December night as he leaned on the door of Bruce's car. She had thought his eyes were dark; instead they were a tawny brown. His hair and the full but limp moustache were something the shade of a sorrel horse.

I've hardly given a thought to Bruce all day. I've been thinking about our do-it-yourself play. I wouldn't think of him now if seeing Jake didn't remind me of him.

"Are you just on your way home from the U, Jake?"

"I'm on my way home from work. I've got a job at the Jewish Hospital."

"Aren't you going to school?"

"I had to drop out, little one. All except for the painting classes and doing the mural at the Student Union. That last raise in tuition did it. I'm on the GI Bill."

"I didn't know you were in the army."

"In Vietnam," he said briefly. "No, Uncle Sam's check just wouldn't stretch—not for paints and canvas and brushes for fixing up my cabin in the hills and a few hamburgers for me. So I got a mop-and-bucket job at the hospital. I'm hoping to be promoted to the kitchen where the food is."

"Oh," Stacy said, and then, "Did you get Aunt Vinia's picture glued up the way it ought to be?"

He stared at her blankly out of his yellowish-brown eyes. "Aunt Vinia's pic—? Good lord! No, I didn't. I'm glad you reminded me. I've got about an hour—and I'll hustle myself right over there and do it."

"I'd like to go with you, Jake."

His smile was the kind that lit up his face and also showed the deep creases in it. "Sure, sure, sugar. Come right along. Could you spare another cupcake? I don't get paid till the fifteenth."

"Take two. They're small," she told him, laughing.

He finished them off while they walked to his parked station wagon, that high red rectangle Stacy had noticed in the parking lot last December twenty-third. It too looked faded and hard used in the bright sunshine.

She asked as he hoisted her up into the high seat, "Would you mind swinging by our house first? I won't be but a minute, and I can drop off my load."

"Wouldn't mind a bit."

With a loud rasping of gears and a bucking start, he headed toward Hubbell Street. Stacy not only dropped off the bakery goods and her books in the kitchen, but pelted up the stairs and took the turquoise necklace out of the top drawer of the bureau she shared with Jill. She would put the question about the return of the gift to Aunt Vinia herself, instead of to Emily Post.

At Aunt Vinia's narrow brick house, the shrill barking sounded again when Jake pressed the old-fashioned round button of the doorbell. Again the door was opened a wary crack before Aunt Vinia swung it wide on her callers. This time also she had on an apron but her hair was not in kid curlers. Involuntarily she put up her hand to cover a sizable bruise on her cheek, so close to her eye that it was bloodshot and blackened.

"What'd the other fellow look like?" Jake asked her.

"Never mind, never mind," she said flusteredly.

"You can always say you bumped into the door," he went on.

"It wasn't a door. It was the newel-post here. I got up the other night to let Butch out. You'd think I'd know by now when I was on the bottom step, instead of thinking I had reached the floor. I sort of lost my balance. I don't know why a little bruise would turn all shades of the rainbow. I've been dosing it with all sorts of salve."

"Get a little chunk of steak," Jake advised, "and, instead of feeding it to Butch, plaster it tight over your eye. That'll help."

"Never mind, never mind," she repeated. "Come on in and sit down."

"You two sit down," he said. "I'm going to stick your picture tight to the window. I should have done it long ago so it wouldn't bulge and droop the way it does."

But Stacy did not sit down. She stood embarrassed and ill at ease. She pulled the velvet box containing the necklace out of her blazer pocket. "Aunt Vinia, I didn't feel right about—I mean, about keeping this necklace you gave me."

"Why? Is something the matter with it?"

"Oh no, no. I just love it. It's the prettiest one I ever had. Only when you gave it to me—"

"You mean you were Bruce's girl then, and you're not now. I heard about that." She added grimly, "She's not my own flesh-and-blood niece. Winifred, Bruce's mother, isn't. She was my husband's niece. She stayed with us for two terms of school. Even then she was a conniver. Always an ax to grind. And it's grown on her. She thinks she can manipulate people like so many puppets. I'd like to see her get her comeuppance one of these days."

Stacy said nothing, but stood fingering the velvet box. Aunt Vinia's eyes came back to her, and the grimness left her face. Her old veined hands pressed Stacy's fingers tighter about the box. "You keep it, dearie. I want you to have it. Yes, and you wear it. Wear it, and catch another boy that isn't as namby-pamby as Bruce. He hasn't come near me lately. I don't wonder. He knows I'd tell him what I thought of him."

"He's busy with basketball."

They talked against the soft background of Jake's brush, brush of glue on the thin paper of the picture. He had put it on the floor of the landing where he could kneel over it. Presently he called to Stacy, "Come here now and hold it at the bottom so I can get it up even."

She held it in place at the two lower corners while he patted and smoothed it firmly to the glass with the palms of his hands. What bony workaday hands they were! The mop he used at the Jewish Hospital must be a self-wringing one, because there were still paint smears on them.

They both backed away from the window, and he

said, "There's your old boy, Aunt Vinia. No wrinkles except the few around his eyes where they're supposed to be."

She too surveyed it and gave a soft chuckle. "I think you're right, Stacy, about his being the saint of the impossible. I asked him to keep Winifred away until my black eye disappeared. And so far he has. Oh, but she'd make a big deal out of it, and how a woman my age has no business living alone. How I could fall, and no one would find me for days—"

Jake interrupted with mock gravity, "I didn't know the old fellow here was responsible for getting Bruce's mother out of town. I thought it was the League of Women Voters that sent her to Washington as a delegate. She'll be gone two weeks. So you can rest easy, Aunt Vinia."

Stacy laughed. "But St. Jude could have nudged the Women Voters to send her, couldn't he?"

They left after having listened to Aunt Vinia's insistence that they come again when they had time to sit down and drink some of her grape juice and after having given her their assurance that they would. Again Stacy sat beside Jake on the high seat of imitation leather with the stuffing coming out at the seams.

This meeting with Jake, this seeing Aunt Vinia, brought back all too vividly that other meeting when life and love had seemed flawless. Hunting for something to start the conversation with, she asked, "Did Allegra get her job at the pancake house? Remember, you were taking her to see about it."

"She got it. She's still there." He pushed a dark lock

of hair back from one eye. "Old long-legged Allegra," he mused. "I was hungry, and she fed me—and lost her job doing it. She's one of the pure in heart that the Bible tells us are blessed. Why, honeypot, that gal can go through all the slime and filth in the world, and come out smiling and loving and untouched. Something like a duck that sheds water. It's a special gift only one in a million have."

"I guess I don't have it," Stacy faltered.

"No, your skin is too thin." He wove his way through traffic on the Boulevard, then asked gently, "What hurt you the most about breaking off with Bruce?"

"I—don't—know."

She had even asked herself that. The gap of loneliness was filling in. She had *almost* ceased to lift her eyes to see if the copper-colored car was waiting in St. Jude's driveway. And no one could be moodily depressed on that ride home in Obie's packed hearse with the wild hilarity of the passengers when the seats tilted and rocked as corners were turned. But there was still that indigestible lump. . . .

She tried to laugh. "Maybe it's just wounded pride because he preferred his mother's car to me."

"Maybe it's disillusionment in the guy because he hasn't grown up."

She longed to ask, Did he say anything to you about our breaking up? Instead she said, "Do—do you ever see him?"

"Not much. He's giving his all to basketball. And I'm giving my all to the mural I'm doing in the Student

Union. I didn't like the first one I started. When it was half done, I painted it out and began over."

Stacy said politely as he turned onto Hubbell Street, "I'd like to see it."

"They're planning a grand opening flingding around St. Patrick's Day. Complete with green punch, dancing, and inspirational speeches. Did you know that a picture if it's worth the space it takes up has something to tell you? It has to make you think something, or feel something—or stir up your insides."

"I never thought of it like that before, Jake. Will your picture stir up people's insides?"

"I hope to God it does. I'm wasting a lot of time and paint if it doesn't."

With that, he stopped at the side of the Belford house, and Stacy, the velvet box containing the turquoise necklace still in her pocket, climbed out.

8 ❧

S T. P A T R I C K' S Day came on Saturday this year.

The dance to celebrate the opening of the enlarged
and redecorated Student Union—the flingding as Jake
called it—would be held on Friday, the night before.
Katie Rose was to come home to go to it with Miguel.

Miguel was an indifferent dancer and the university
he attended was thirty miles away. But Salvadore, a boy
he had known in Mexico who was now an art major
here, had painted one of the murals on the Student
Union wall. The loyal Miguel had promised Salvadore
he would be at the opening to see it.

After much phoning back and forth to Bannon, it
was arranged that Grandda O'Byrne would drive Katie
Rose home on Friday afternoon and stay the weekend.

Saturday night would be the big night for the Belfords. Even though Guido, the balding and bouncy
proprietor of the Gay Nineties, had come from Italy he
always put on a program at his nightclub in honor of
the Irish saint. For the past few years, the program had

been provided by Mother at the piano with Ben, Katie Rose, and Stacy doing the song and dance numbers. For this gala evening a table was set up at the Gay Nineties for the whole Belford family and any friends they cared to invite.

Much discussion took place in the Belford home about these *two* St. Patrick's Day celebrations. Jeanie Kincaid, who had a finger in many pies at the U, would also go to the Student Union one. "I'm to cover it for the paper," she boasted.

But Ben, who was sandwich man at the Ragged Robin on the evening shift and had arranged to have Saturday night off to participate in the festivities at the Gay Nineties, didn't dare ask for Friday as well.

"That's all right," Jeanie told him with her amiable crinkly smile. "I'll go there early on my own. Then you can come after me when you get off from work."

Stacy was *not* going to the Student Union affair—either early or late. She cringed at the very thought of it. For surely Bruce would break off his rigid basketball training long enough to take Joyce Black-something to it. His mother would see to that, no doubt.

Jeanie had enlightened them more on the Student Union party. No, not everyone would wear Irish costumes. "Oh, I imagine there'll be some plug hats and shillelaghs. But the girls will just dress in whatever they have that's green. No one will go all out for it. So tell Katie Rose to save her green kilts and lacy blouse for Guido's."

Thereupon Mother rummaged through her old cedar chest where she stored the articles she bought at rummage sales, because they were bargains even though she had no immediate need for them. The dirt-cheap box, the family called her chest. In it she found a summery dress with a green top, full white skirt, and gold belt she had brought home last fall.

"Just like new," Mother said. "Though I suppose Katie Rose will turn her nose up at it."

(Katie Rose not only did not like other people to wear her clothes; she hated wearing anything that anyone else, either known or unknown, had worn before.)

Stacy came home from school on Thursday to find her mother seated at the portable sewing machine on the dinette table. She stopped her stitching to explain, "I'm making this for Miguel. He phoned to ask if we didn't have an Irish vest he could wear to the dance tomorrow night, and I told him yes. But I looked and looked for that one we have. Someone must have borrowed it and never brought it back. So I found this green satin. I suppose I got it at a rummage sale—"

Stacy chortled. "No supposing about it."

"We'll have to have green buttons for it. Would you mind, love, going to the dime store to get them? If they're only four on a card, get two cards. Oh, and see if they'd have a green belt for Katie Rose to wear with her dress—you know, instead of that gold one."

Mother got up, hunted for her purse, and took a bill from it. For a moment she stood there holding it, looking dubiously at Stacy. Then she said, "I have a message for you. At first I thought—Well, I didn't know whether to tell you—but she'll probably call again."

"Who?"

"A couple of days ago a woman phoned and asked for you. I said you hadn't come home from school yet, and asked her if she wanted to leave a message. But she said no, she'd call again."

"Don't you know who it was?"

"Just wait. Then today she called again—about half an hour ago. It was the same woman. When I told her you weren't home yet, she wanted to know when I expected you, and I said I didn't know because you had started practicing for your school play. And this time when I said I'd have you call back if she'd leave her name, she did." Mother's laugh was both uneasy and angry. "It was her majesty herself—the one you said had on a minx jacket, and I said No, it was a minx in a mink jacket."

Stacy could only stare at her mother. Bruce's mother calling *her*. Suddenly it seemed hard for her to catch her breath; she felt as though all the oxygen had left the room. "What'd she want?" she murmured.

"She wouldn't say. She just said if you came home in the next half hour to call her back." Mother picked up the green vest, turned it over, and without looking at Stacy's drained face, asked, "Don't you want to call her back?"

"Heavens, no! I certainly do not want to call her back. If she calls again, tell her she's the last person on earth I'd call back."

"Don't think I won't! Her and her snooty *grande-dame* airs. 'I'd appreciate if you'd have Stacy return my call,'" she added in mincing tones.

"I'll get the buttons," Stacy said.

"Here, take a sample of this green satin. Don't worry if they aren't a perfect match. As Gran would say, 'It'll never show when you're milking a cow.'" She tried to laugh, but broke off to say anxiously, "Oh, my dear own, don't worry about that minx in her mink jacket."

"She's the least of my worries," Stacy almost shouted. *Bruce's mother calling her!*

On the Boulevard, she bought the green buttons at the dime store. She found a green belt too which would fit Katie Rose, she knew, because she tried it on.

She came out, and was just passing the Pantages movie house when she caught a glimpse of a small resolute figure in a brown tweed suit walking down the street toward her. Oh, no—oh, no! The late afternoon was not chilly enough for a fur jacket. It was carried over her arm.

Stacy swiftly turned her back to the street, pressed herself close to the recessed doors of the theater, and stared through the glass at the refreshment counter inside. With straining ears, she listened to the oncoming click of heels, praying that they would click right past her.

Instead, with a small rustle of paper packages, a hand was laid on her arm, and a voice said, "Stacy! What luck running into you here." And then a volley of words about having tried desperately to get in touch with her, but that Stacy seemed to be a very busy young lady. . . .

Stacy backed away a step, holding with both hands

the gray envelope of her purchases in front of her like a shield. "What did you want to talk to me about?" she asked bluntly. *What ax do you have to grind now?*

"There's something I would so like to talk over with you. Something I'm very troubled about. I can't help thinking that *you* would be more understanding than anyone. Couldn't we stop in someplace—maybe Downey's Drugstore—for a cup of coffee? Only I guess you young people prefer Coke."

"I don't have time. Mom sent me to get some buttons, and she's waiting for them."

"Please, Stacy. It'd be a great favor to me." Honest pleading had taken the place of effusiveness. After her second "Please, my dear, it won't take long," Stacy said, "All right. Downey's is right here."

They took the first booth in the drugstore. Stacy tried not to glance at the corner one where she had sat so often with Bruce on their good days and bad. The coffee-vending machine was crowded close to the newspaper rack. Customers were supposed to fill their own paper cups and help themselves to the miniature envelopes of sugar and powdered cream. But Mrs. Seerie had only settled herself in the booth with her few oddments of purchases. *I'm not about to rush up and get her coffee for her.*

The woman said with a sigh, "I've been up and down the Boulevard getting all the little last-minute things for our St. Patrick's Day party at the Children's Hospital."

"A party for the children?"

"Oh, no, for our board." Another sigh. "I thought

when I got out of the cast and the sling that my broken collarbone would be as good as new again. But I still tire so easily, and I get a throbbing ache in my right shoulder."

That remark called for an "Oh, I'm sorry" from Stacy, but she failed to make it.

The druggist's wife came to their table. She spoke to Stacy and asked about her mother. Evidently Bruce's mother wasn't known to her for she only gave her a trade smile and asked what she'd like.

"Coffee," said Mrs. Seerie. "Black."

"I'll get my Coke," Stacy said, glad to escape from the booth for a moment or two.

She brought the opened bottle back to where the woman waited with her coffee now in front of her. Stacy asked again, "What did you want to talk to me about?"

Mrs. Seerie didn't answer that, but started a dissertation on how parents only wanted to do what was right for their children. They constantly thought of a child's future happiness. . . .

The good old routine. Stacy listened, her eyes fixed on the popcorn flicking merrily behind the glass walls of its machine. Bruce had always bought her popcorn, and she had always wheedled Mr. Downey into putting an extra spurt of butter on it. Her eyes, seeking a more neutral spot, moved to the rack of candies and nuts in cellophane envelopes. The coughdrops were at the top of the tier. Bruce had bought those for her too when she had been hoarse after cheerleading at a St. Jude's football game. *"I want to shelter you from all turmoil, and all I can do is buy you coughdrops.*"

She fastened shaky fingers around the Coke bottle and took a deep drink from it. It was all so cock-eyed —her sitting here opposite this woman who had never liked her, instead of with her son who had told her she was the only girl he could ever care for.

"No one is more cognizant of the terrible unrest among the young people today than Bruce's father and I. But we never thought Bruce. . . ." His mother was folding the square of paper napkin into a triangle, and then folding that into a smaller triangle which she had to hold down with her fingers. "I went to Washington as a delegate. I decided, as long as I was so close to New York, I'd run up and see some plays. I've really had my nose close to the grindstone for so long."

Your nose and your ax, her listener amended silently.

"And when I came home, I couldn't believe—I simply couldn't believe the change in Bruce. You haven't seen him lately, have you?"

"Not since early in January."

"I simply can't understand his going so completely off the deep end."

Stacy wanted to cry out, "You mean he's gone off the deep end over Joyce?" Instead she said in a flat voice, "He must be pretty busy with basketball practice and games—and keeping up his grades."

"Oh, no, my dear. He hasn't carried through with basketball the way the coach expected—and hoped. He doesn't even go out for practice. I asked him if it was his knee—you know he has what they call a football

(95)

knee. But he said it had nothing to do with his knee—that all he had to do was to tape it tight and he never knew he had it. I asked his father to reason with him. Bruce wouldn't listen. He shows his father no respect these days."

Stacy sat wordless. Mrs. Seerie was now folding the square of napkin into a tight rectangle. "He spends a lot of his time at Jake's place"—her small laugh was tinged with apology—"I know parents have a way of blaming their children's misdemeanors on the influence of others, but I can't help thinking Jake is responsible for Bruce's changed attitude. Jake is older; he's been in the war. Maybe you know him?"

"Yes, I know him." She had an instant's picture of his shabbiness and gauntness, and she wondered if he'd been promoted to the hospital kitchen where the food was. He'd been sweet and teasing with Aunt Vinia, and understanding to the girl who'd ridden with him in the red Volks station wagon to see her.

"He's doing a mural on the Student Union wall," Stacy volunteered.

"Yes, I've heard he's a promising painter, but he has an artist's disregard for the—the worthwhile attainments in life. And he's passing that on to Bruce, so that I—I can't reach him at all."

The chill trembling had moved from Stacy's hands to her middle. So Bruce was no longer so firmly under his parents' thumb as he had always been. *But why is she telling me all this?*

As though the woman had heard her unuttered question, she pushed her well-creased napkin aside and said, "I wondered if you—because you and Bruce always got along so beautifully—if you wouldn't help him get back on the right track."

"Me—I mean, I?" A short laugh exploded from her. "I thought you had a girl named Joyce all set up for Bruce. Why doesn't she get him back on the right track?"

Bruce's mother gave an airy self-deprecatory laugh. "Live and learn, I find. I guess parents have to find out the hard way that they can't choose dates for their children. It was only that the Blackwells had moved here from Kansas City, so that their daughter didn't know any of the young people on campus and I thought—"

Stacy broke in coldly, "Did you and Mr. Seerie talk this over and decide there were worse things than Bruce's going with me? And is Mr. Seerie waiting for you to report back to him?"

"No, Mr. Seerie— That is, he's been very busy lately." For a brief second Stacy saw the bleak look that flickered across the woman's face before she picked up her intimate just-us-two-women-together smile. "Oh, no, Stacy. No, this little talk with you was my idea. I don't know what caused you and Bruce to break up . . ."

You were the what and the why and even the when. As though you don't know!

And now the smile was quite arch. "But I know it would take only a word from you. That isn't asking too much, is it, my dear?"

So that was it. The club president had finally got

down to the nitty-gritty and put the motion before the house. All in favor say Aye. Bruce's mother, after adroitly pushing her out of the picture, was now seeking to bring her back to help get Bruce into line. What a laugh.

The store had become more crowded. Mr. Downey turned up the volume of the TV set on the wall in back of the soda fountain so that customers could better hear the four-thirty weather report and newscast. Many of them lingered to hear it.

A male voice announced, "Our balmy days are ended. Weather forecasters tell us a storm, bringing snow and a drop in temperature, is sweeping in from the northwest."

A customer in the store quoted with wise headshakings, "February fair, in March beware."

The voice continued, "Already mountain roads are covered with sleety snow and motorists are warned—"

Mrs. Seerie bent over the table to murmur confidingly, "Stacy, you'd only have to phone Bruce. Or supposing I tell him you *have* phoned and want him to call you—"

A strangled *No* came from Stacy. "No, I wouldn't be a party to such a—such a sneaky deal."

What did the Seeries think she was anyway? A pawn on a chessboard to be shoved either forward or back? First, Bruce and his scheme of pulling the wool over his parents' eyes by their meeting at Jake's. And now this woman wanting her to pull the same dirty wool over Bruce's eyes.

She took another swallow of Coke, hoping it would calm her inner shakiness. It didn't. She stood up. "I have to get home with these buttons for Miguel Parnell's vest so he can wear it to the St. Patrick's dance tomorrow night."

"You mean the St. Patrick's dance out on campus— the one to open the new Student Union?"

Stacy nodded. "Miguel's taking my sister Katie Rose."

Mrs. Seerie's eyes brightened. "Oh, yes, the son of the noted writer. He's a friend of Bruce's. Wait, Stacy, wait. That's another thing that—well, it alarms me. There's this girl named Allegra hanging around Jake's place. She was always phoning Bruce until I put a stop to it—the cheap brazen little piece."

But Jake had called Allegra life's stepchild and one of the pure in heart. She had fed him when he was hungry, and had lost her job doing it.

"From what I gather," the voice across the table went on, "she wants to go to the dance with Jake and Bruce. You can see, can't you, my dear, that a girl like that simply isn't the type a boy should take to a university function?"

Still no answer from Stacy. The woman's lips which had thinned at mention of Allegra were now shaped into an ingratiating—even wheedling—smile. "Suppose I mention to Bruce that I saw you and you mentioned that your sister and Michael Parnell—"

"Miguel."

The airy laugh again. "That's right. I keep forgetting

that Bruce always calls him Miguel. It would be so easy for me just to mention that you'd like to go to the dance."

"No, no, do you hear me!" Stacy leaned over the table and said as emphatically as she could without being overheard by the TV viewers, "If you tell him that, I'll tell him you lied." If only her voice wasn't so wobbly. "I have to go." She turned back to mutter, "Thanks for the Coke."

She wished, as she dodged through traffic crossing the Boulevard and started toward Hubbell Street, that she hadn't let her enemy pay for the Coke. It was as though her stomach knew it. And she knew by the growing feeling inside her that it wasn't going to stay down.

The Belford family said that Stacy grieved with her stomach. When anything churned up her heart, her stomach also started churning. Three blocks from home, holding on to a prickly hedge that served as a fence around a white house with green shutters, she parted with the Coke.

9 ⤬

T_{HE} predicted storm swooped down from the north the next day around noontime. During the first afternoon class at St. Jude's, word came over the P.A. system that because of the storm Sister Therese was canceling the seniors' afterschool meeting. It was at this meeting that the class was to have talked over and voted on which student should take which part in *The Song of Bernadette.*

The wind-driven sleet caught Stacy like a brutal slap in the face as she pushed through the heavy oak doors at the end of school. Even so, she told Obie, "I won't ride home with you in the hearse today. I want to walk in the snow."

"Snow! Why, bless your indomitable soul, this is a March blizzard."

She tightened the scarf under her chin and turned up her coat collar. "That's okay. I like walking in a blizzard too."

"So be it, ice maiden. If you're not at school Monday, we'll send out the Saint Bernard with a keg of booze around his neck."

She wasn't sure why she wanted to walk alone in the storm. At least, snow that pelted the face and wind that whipped under coat and skirt were something tangible to battle, whereas that meeting in the drugstore yesterday had been shadowboxing.

Her mind and heart were still a confused hodgepodge. Surely Bruce's mother was exaggerating. "I wouldn't trust her as far as I could throw an elephant," she muttered without opening her lips because she didn't want to get a mouthful of snow. Just because Bruce didn't yes-mama–no-papa them the way he always had didn't mean he had gone off the deep end. She, Stacy, could even take vicious satisfaction in his lack of respect for his father. And hurray, hurray, if his mother wasn't able to reach him. But his throwing over basketball? And Allegra always phoning him?

Why did that woman—damn her eyes!—have to stir up all the old hurt and rancor, just when Stacy was beginning to push it into a corner of her being and concentrate on poor badgered Bernadette with her unshaken faith? . . . Could it be—could it possibly be—that Bruce had ceased to be the donkey following the carrot?

Snow-coated and chilled to the marrow, she reached her own corner on Hubbell Street. There sat Miguel Parnell's small car which she recognized under its marshmallow frosting of snow.

She was no sooner inside the house, before she could even stamp and shake off the snow, than she was surrounded by the littles shouting the latest news. "Miguel came. But guess what? Katie Rose can't get in to go to the dance with him. Grandda phoned and said he wasn't jackass enough to drive fifty-seven miles when he couldn't see his hand in front of his face."

Brian added with his grave smile, "Gran wouldn't draw an easy breath if he did."

And there was Miguel sitting at the dinette table drinking tea. He greeted Stacy with his bright chipmunk grin. "I was afraid Petunia couldn't make it down through the storm. But I came anyway because I told Salvadore I would. So I'll take you to the dance, *petit chou.*"

"Oh, no!" *Oh, no! Not when Bruce would surely be there—not with Joyce, but with Allegra.*

"Why not?" Mother said. "Take off your boots, and here's a cup of hot tea for you. Yes, go with Miguel. You'll look pretty in that green and white dress. I pressed it. And you'll meet a lot of nice boys."

She meant, as Stacy knew, that maybe she would meet a nice boy who would take Bruce's place in her life. Only then would Mother draw that easy breath Gran was always referring to.

"*Somebody* has to wear the corsage Miguel bought," Jill said. "*Green* carnations."

"But I won't know anyone there."

"I should know plenty of people," Miguel said. "I'm no treat to dance with, but I'll try to drag up some good partners for you."

"Jeanie will be there too," Mother said, "and she can help introduce you around."

(*103*)

Well, why not? Since when did she have to dodge Bruce Seerie? This might be her chance to find out if his mother was making much out of nothing. And if she wasn't, if Allegra with the wide loving smile was part of his going off the deep end, why fine—just fine. Then she could close the door with a bang on her past with Bruce. No more looking back. No more nagging tag ends of wondering if the strong he-man Bruce might be waiting for her some afternoon at St. Jude's in a car that wasn't his mother's.

"Okay. I'll wear the green carnations and go."

Afterward when Claire asked her whether people had worn Irish costumes and whether the Student Union had new draperies and furniture, Stacy could only answer vaguely, "I didn't notice."

"For Pat's sake, you've got eyes in your head, haven't you?"

But from the moment Stacy walked in the door with Miguel, the eyes in her head whether she wanted them to or not had been used for only one thing—for searching through the crowd for a glimpse of a deep-chested stalwart boy with dark good looks and hazel eyes under a clinging mat of black hair.

Miguel was a good escort. He took off her coat, shook the snow from it, and gave it to the girl behind the improvised checking stand. He helped her off with her boots and on with Katie Rose's green pumps, which he had carried for her, each wadded into a pocket of his parka. Then he guided her through the milling crowd of young people to locate his friend's mural.

They stopped before it. It was of two small Mexican children, each holding an empty bowl. Their heads were large and out of proportion to their wispy bodies, their great, sad, appealing eyes out of proportion to their wan faces.

"What does Salvadore's picture say to you, Stacy?" Miguel asked.

"I don't know—except that I want to cry."

"It says *hunger*. Lord, those poor little scavengers down there. Sometimes at night I think about them. I dream about going back with a whole basketfull of dollar bills and tossing them out—you know, like you toss popcorn to the ducks on the lake in the park."

"I'd like to fill their bowls with Mom's Irish stew."

But even then, even after he introduced her to Salvadore and the three of them stood talking, her eyes kept roving through the crowd. The dancing had started now.

She danced one dance with Miguel, but he was the kind who liked talking to people better than dancing. They had started on the second one when he stopped and said, "There's our Jeanie. Come on. Let's see what she has to say."

Jeanie Kincaid was skirting the small dance space, holding a pad and pencil and looking her usual bright-eyed self. "I'm supposed to make intelligent notes on the murals," she told them. "And then one of the refreshment committee couldn't show up on account of the snow, so I'm filling in for her too. That's a job in it-self. I mean, trying to keep boys with bottles from spik-ing the punch so it would burn your tonsils out."

"If you see any unattached men, introduce them to Stacy," Miguel said, "so she won't be stuck dancing with me all night."

"There won't be a lot of dancing. We have to leave time for the speeches," Jeanie said.

Stacy was wondering if she could ask Jeanie very cas-ually, "Have you seen Bruce Seerie?" when Jeanie went scurrying off.

But at the end of Stacy's third dance with Miguel, Jeanie came squeezing her way back through the crowd with a sandy-haired boy in tow. She introduced him as Claude McIntosh. "He's been clutching my elbow and wanting to meet you, Stacy. He has too nice manners to butt in."

Miguel, always interested in what a person was ma-joring in and what his plans for the future were, struck up a conversation with the boy who was in Jeanie's speech class. Jeanie drew Stacy aside to say under cover of the rock band, "He's a regular Alger hero. He's a young man with a goal," She added meaning-fully, "Maybe he isn't the athletic hero type like some I could mention, but at least he's on his own with no parents breathing down his neck."

"From what I hear the athletic hero isn't an athletic hero anymore, and he'll have none of his parents' breathing down his neck," Stacy answered.

"I've heard rumors of that too. I have to leap back to

the punchbowl and guard it from the boys with bottles."

Miguel said with a fatherly wave of his hand, "Go ahead and dance, you two."

Claude McIntosh was a little on the short side. The eyes under the sandy hair were light blue and very alert. He danced with little give to him as though his joints needed oiling.

And how he talked. He was taking Business Ad, had one more year to go. He had put himself through school without taking a dime from his folks. They owned and ran a grain elevator in a little town over on the Western Slope, and they didn't see any sense in higher education. They thought he ought to be content to weigh in grain and pray that the price would go up before he had to sell. But not he, Claude. Right now he was crowding in a job, selling shoes in a downtown department store, and carrying a full load besides. He wanted to learn all there was to learn about merchandising.

They were passing the long refreshment table, and Stacy murmured, "Oh, there's the green punch I've been hearing about."

"Let's stop and try it," he said amiably.

A few people fringed the long table with its green decorations. A punch bowl sat at each end with plates of cookies and green mints in between. Miguel and Jeanie were standing to one side talking, and they both smiled at Stacy—Miguel with his benign bless-you-my-children one, and Jeanie with a lifted eyebrow that asked for her, How do you like your young man with a goal?

Stacy smiled back dubiously. Claude pushed his determined way to the punch bowl, and a girl filled the two glass cups he held out. Stacy took a thirsty gulp of hers and gave a strangled cough. Boys with bottles had certainly done things to it.

Another girl across the table was helping herself to a generous handful of cookies. She looked over at Stacy and laughed. "Tastes like what you spray hen coops with, doesn't it?" She laughed again, a joyous childlike laugh. "You're Stacy. Remember me—Allegra? Remember I was at Jake's that night you stopped with Bruce way back in December?"

Stacy blinked her watering eyes. "Of course, I remember. Hi, Allegra."

Way back in December Jake had called her life's stepchild. Just yesterday Mrs. Seerie had called her a cheap brazen little piece. And right now one of the college girls behind the punch bowl, who was discreetly dressed in a long green velvet skirt and immaculate white blouse, flicked a disdainful eye over Allegra who had taken a moment away from her enjoyable crunching of cookies to pull a much-stretched, machine-crocheted, yellowish-green slipover back onto her shoulder.

Evidently striving to wear a suitable costume for a St. Patrick's Day party, Allegra was also attired in a very grassy-green silk skirt. It puckered around the waist, but was strained tight over her sizable hips and behind. She must have made it herself, Stacy thought, feeling a wave of compassion for her and resentment toward the punch ladler whose eyes were now taking in Allegra's straggly bangs.

Her guess proved correct, for Allegra came around the table, snatching another handful of cookies as she did so, and moved close enough to ask in a low voice, "Stacy, do you happen to have a safety pin? I made this skirt out of the lining in a coat my landlady gave me, and I was in such a hurry I didn't sew the hem in well enough. It's ripping out." She extended a long leg, turning it to show where the hem wasn't holding. "See? And if I dance, it'll just rip more and more."

"No, I don't have a safety pin or even a straight one." But because she wanted nothing more than to help, Stacy unclasped the green-enameled shamrock pin from her blouse. "Here, why can't we use this one?"

"Landsakes, honey, that's your St. Patrick one."

"It's just dime store. Hold still a minute." Stacy bent down and fastened the bit of sagging hem with the shamrock pin.

Allegra looked down at it with preening pleasure. "That's swell, Stacy. It looks as if it was meant to be a St. Patrick's decoration. You're swell too," she said, and threw her arms around Stacy. Then she reached for a handful of green mints. "Um-mm, wintergreen. Here, take some. I'm having the best time."

She turned to call out loudly, "Jake! Hey, Jake, now I can dance."

(109)

Jake detached himself from a knot of fellows and came over. He gave Allegra a laughing push away from the table. "Stop champing down all the food, farm girl, or you'll disgrace us all." He turned his face-creasing grin on Stacy. "And you, little sugar candy, have got to see my picture. If you don't like it, I'll clobber you."

10 ❧

TONIGHT Jake's shapeless tweed jacket with the leather patches at the elbows seemed to hang even more loosely on him than it had before. Maybe that was because his checked flannel shirt had been replaced by a white one, which wasn't as white as it should be.

"Did you get promoted to the kitchen yet?" Stacy asked him.

"On Thursdays and Fridays. Then I get to fill trays and myself." He took her arm and said peremptorily, "Come along with me."

She glanced back as she was piloted along. Allegra was still relishing her wintergreen mints, and the sandy-haired boy named Claude was looking after them a trifle resentfully.

Jake stopped in front of one of the murals. "Here's my baby. Turn your bright green eyes on it."

At first glance, Jake's picture seemed all gaudy blobs, yet there was a sobering something about it too. A background—not clearly drawn but suggested—of upraised arms, of chains being broken, and doors being smashed. In the center, Stacy saw as she edged closer, was a fluffy yellow chicken emerging from its shell. Not knowing exactly what comment to make, she said, "Your chicken has more expression on its face than any new-hatched chick I ever saw."

"What sort of expression would you say?"

"Oh, kind of bewildered and hopeful and—scared, I guess. And those grayish ovals that look like unhatched eggs—Are they eggs too that the chicks haven't broken out of yet?"

"You're smart, sugar. How do you know so much about chickens breaking out of their shells?

"Gran O'Byrne sets hens and hatches them every spring."

"Yes, the grayish eggs are the ones where the little chicks inside thought to themselves, 'It's nice and warm and protected in here, so why break the shell and get out in the cold?' "

"But they die if they don't."

"Righto. If the light was better, you'd see the dead ones inside. And, yes, my new-hatched one is bewildered and scared. That's what I wanted to show—that the human chicks breaking out of chains and locked doors, are kind of scared too. That's why all the marches and protests are done in great numbers. That's why when they run away from home they go straight to some pad that's crowded with others. Because we know—at least the ones who use their heads—that freedom isn't free. You pay a high price for smashing old traditions and authority."

She felt the gravity of the tall, slightly stooped boy beside her. He went on, "This is the breaking out of the shell, the saying No to what we *don't* want in life. And then I'm going to do another, and it'll be a companion piece to this one. It'll be the saying Yes to all the things we think we and the world need."

"Like what?"

"Like more *you can,* and less *you can't*. Like more understanding and communication, and less emphasis on money and status. Like more love, and less law. What I want it to be is sort of a Sermon on the Mount for today." His musing smile brushed over her. "You don't need it, honeypot. You're one that was born with love in your heart."

She didn't mean them to, but the words burst from her. "Jake, did Bruce come with you and Allegra?"

"Yes, he's here. I had to drag him away from that punch that's been spiked till I could use it for paint remover. You know, Stacy, when a fellow's been brought up on Koolade and with a strong hand on his shoulder —well, when he shakes off the strong hand, he feels he has to prove something to himself and everyone else— though I don't think he knows himself what he's trying to prove."

The sandy-haired Claude was suddenly beside them, saying, "No use letting the music go to waste. They tell me the band is about to quit and the speeches begin." To Jake, he added, "Your girl wants to dance with you."

Stacy's mind was still on Bruce who was trying to prove something. She laid a hand on Jake's arm and again the words were forced from her, "Is Allegra your girl . . . or Bruce's?"

He looked down at her with a quizzical smile. "She comes over and mucks out that dirty hole I live in and sews buttons on my clothes. Please note, buttons." He proudly displayed three buttons on his coat, one of which didn't match. "She brews up strong coffee for Bruce when he goes a little too far in trying to prove whatever he's trying to prove."

"I keep remembering your saying she's one of the pure in heart."

"Yes, one of the unsullied. If this shoe salesman wasn't so impatient, I'd tell you more about it, how the lowdown of the world can never sully her."

Stacy had one final word for him. "Your picture churned up my insides, Jake."

"Did it, sweet? Then it was worth going without bacon to buy brushes."

He shoved his way back to the refreshment table and Allegra. Stacy danced with Claude. It was then she realized what she had only been dimly conscious of before. Her right pump—or rather, Katie Rose's right pump—was pinching unbearably. Maybe if Claude had been the kind who put rhythm and abandon in a dance, she wouldn't have noticed it.

"Claude, would you mind if we sat down somewhere? One of my shoes hurts like crazy."

He obligingly guided her through the dancers. Every couch and chair were already full to overflowing. Even the chairarms were occupied. But two girls on a piano bench moved more tightly together and indicated a half foot of space on which Stacy might perch.

Claude said, "Let's take a look at that slipper." He squatted down on his heels and pulled it off her foot."

In a thoroughly professional way, he lifted her ankle with one hand and measured the sole of the pump against the sole of her foot with the other.

"No wonder it pinches. It's at least a half-size—maybe a whole size—too narrow. Whatever clerk fitted you with these certainly didn't know his business. Tell you what you do. You take them right back to the store where you got them. Don't go to the clerk that waited on you. Go to the manager. You show him what a lousy fit they are, and insist on the store's replacing them. And stick to your guns. Don't let him talk you out of it."

Stacy laughed. "They're not mine. They're my sister's, and her foot is smaller. And besides, there's no taking them back because Mom got them at a rummage sale. For about fifty cents, I suppose."

"She did! And you wear things she buys at rummage sales?" His eyes glowed, and his sudden smile turned his face boyish and likable. "Hey, that's wonderful. I thought maybe you were one of those girls—you know, the kind with a rich dad that just goes down and charges whatever she wants. The school is full of them. Or else they're the far-out kind that thinks hard work and stretching a buck makes you a capitalist—or part of the Establishment."

He stood up, still holding the shoe. "You don't know how relieved I am. You're just the kind of girl I've been looking for. You don't put on airs. I told Jeanie you looked like my dream girl, but I never thought—"

With that, a girl and a boy who had been on the wide arm of an upholstered chair not three feet from Stacy's end of the piano bench stood up and moved off. And Stacy found herself looking into the dark and somewhat blank eyes of the boy who was slumped in the chair's depths. For a breathless moment their eyes locked before she faltered out, "Well, hi, Bruce. Jake said you were here but I—I—" She stopped short of saying I looked all over for you and didn't see you.

He made a futile effort to hoist himself out of the chair. Failing that, he reached out and managed to grab Stacy's wrist. "I want to tell you something, Stacy . . ." His mumbled words came with painstaking effort.

She could only stare at him aghast. This wasn't Bruce—not this sloppy, uncoordinated boy who drooled his words and couldn't get out of the chair.

Claude busied himself putting on her shoe, saying as he did so, "Come on. Let's get out of here."

"What I want to tell you. . . . Now—don't—go 'way —because I've got to tell you—"

"Look, bud, you're not in shape to tell anybody anything right now," Claude said decisively. "Let go her hand."

"Let's see you make me." With a herculean effort and still gripping Stacy's wrist, Bruce thrust himself out of the chair and onto his feet. Very unsteady feet they were, so that his free hand groped for something to hold on to. But he snarled belligerently, "I only need one hand to shut you up. Yeh—just one fist to bash your mug in—"

Stacy looked about in helpless panic. The attention of everyone around them was directed toward the fracas. If she could only free her wrist from the fingers that were clamped upon it and eel away into the crowd. Oh, where was Miguel?

And then she felt the grip slacken and Bruce's hand drop. She looked at him and saw the grayish-green tinge of nausea take over his face. She saw the sudden horror in his unfocused eyes.

Without a word he fled, plunging through the crowd, and like the football player he was, elbowing, straight-arming his way toward the outside door. He was soon lost to her sight. She could only hope he made the door and the snowy darkness in time.

In her letdown shaky state and with Claude still sputtering irately, Miguel's appearance seemed that of a savior. She said weakly, "Let's go home, Miguel."

He brought her boots to her and said, "Shove your tootsies into these. Yes, we'll take off before the dedication speeches start." He very nicely dismissed the young man with a goal. "Thanks a thousand, Claude, for dancing with Stacy. My feet can't seem to follow the music."

Claude shook hands with them both, holding Stacy's a little longer than necessary. "I'll be getting in touch with you," he promised.

She sat in Miguel's low car and shivered while he was brushing the snow off it. She shivered during the short ride home, and even when they were in the house and she had kicked off her wet boots and shed her wraps.

Miguel hunted through the basement and found some cartons which he tore apart. He wadded up newspaper and made a fire of sorts in the fireplace. It was a piddling fire, but even if it had been a roaring one, Stacy was sure she wouldn't have been warmed by it.

She said as they huddled in front of it, "I saw Bruce there tonight."

"I saw him too," he said cryptically. Maybe Mother —or Jeanie—had already briefed him on the Stacy–Bruce affair for he added brightly, "That Claude that stuck to you so close—he seems like a nice fellow. Jeanie was telling me what a good student and hard worker he is."

She unpinned her wilted green corsage. "What's an Alger hero, Miguel? That's what Jeanie called him."

He threw back his head and laughed. "Shades of the past—Horatio Alger. He wrote books about the poor boy with a frank open countenance. Always the strive-and-succeed, the rags-to-riches theme. Alger's young hero was always kind to his mother; he helped old ladies across the street. His clothes were threadbare, but always clean and neatly pressed. Yeh, and he was always at hand to save the banker's beautiful little daughter when the horses ran away with the buggy she was riding in. Gramps had the whole set of them, and when I stayed there one summer, I went through the lot. Phil the Fiddler. Tom the Young Bootblack. Grit the Young Boatman. I soaked them up."

"Maybe that's why you help old ladies across the street."

"Maybe." He chuckled. "Come to think of it, Claude has that frank open countenance, and I have a hunch he'll strive and succeed too. He's a nice guy. He seems like the kind that knows his own mind, and—" He paused as though he wanted to say more.

Maybe he thought of saying, "He'd never be pushed around by his parents. And if he pushed them off, he'd never drink so much loaded punch, he couldn't keep it down." Instead he said, "You go on to bed, *petit chou.* I'll wait till the fire burns down, and then I'll look around for an empty cot."

"It's in Ben's room," she said from the doorway. "Jill and I made it up for you."

In her upstairs room, she hurriedly undressed and climbed into bed beside the warm lump that was Jill. Very gently she tugged enough of the blanket over to cover herself. Heaven forbid that Jill should waken and launch into any part of the Itsy Sullivan saga. This was one night Stacy wanted sleep to come as fast as it could.

11 ～

$T H E$ St. Patrick's Day celebration at Guido's Gay Nineties the following night did much to smooth Stacy's crumpled spirits.

Guido was at the door to greet the Belford family and to present them each with a green carnation. For Mother, who had many admirers, there were two green orchid corsages, and a basket of white roses lavish with green ribbon waited upon the piano. Many of the diners had heard and watched the Irish songs and dances on previous years, and they clapped their welcome as the head waiter escorted the Belfords to their table.

In deference to the saint who had chased the snakes out of Ireland, the waiters with handle-bar mustaches were wearing green shirts, instead of their usual red-checked ones. The red-checked tablecloths too were replaced by ones as grassy green as the skirt Allegra had worn the night before. Green lasagna, made by Guido's mother, was featured on the menu.

"Just wait till I tell Cathie Ott *I* was at a nightclub and had a green carnation and green noodles," Jill bragged.

"Does Mrs. Guido really put alfalfa in them?" Brian asked Miguel.

"It's almost worse—spinach."

With the storm's abating, Katie Rose had come down from Bannon not with Grandda O'Byrne—there were still Gran's uneasy breaths to be considered—but on the bus. Miguel had stayed over for the gala night. And Ben had brought Jeanie, who sat at the table between him and Matt, wearing the Irish kilts she had made last year for this same occasion, with her cinnamon-brown eyes sparkling.

The program led off with Mother playing "The Irish Washerwoman" and Katie Rose, Ben, and Stacy dancing an Irish jig to it. And next the prime favorite, "Cockles and Mussels, Alive, Alive-O." As usual when they came to "Through streets broad and narrow/I pushed the wheelbarrow . . . ," Ben imitated a wheelbarrow by throwing himself onto his hands and Katie Rose took his feet and pushed him along. That always brought a loud burst of applause.

Stacy felt her old joie de vivre surge through her. Later—later on—she would sort out the jumble of emotions that roiled inside her. Later she would summon anger so that she could say to herself, "If Bruce has something he's dying to tell me, he knows where I live. Claude was right, he wasn't fit to tell anybody anything." But it was hard to forget—harder not to feel sorry for a boy who had had to make such a hasty and ignominious plunge for the outdoors.

People came to the Belfords' table to ask for requests, or they shouted them from distant tables. Katie Rose sang her special song, a lesser-known ballad Uncle Brian had taught her: "You Hold My Heart in Your Two Little Hands."

An old gentleman at a table in a far corner kept demanding "When Irish Eyes Are Smiling." Mother nodded to Stacy. "You sing it love. And stand close to his table, in case he's a little deaf." The violinist accompanied the piano while Stacy sang, "In the lilt of Irish laughter/You can hear the angels sing. . . ."

As she wended her way back to the piano, a man got up from his table and caught her arm. "Wait a minute, sister. I just want to tell you that you sing like a meadowlark."

"Oh, thanks. We always put on the St. Patrick's show for Guido."

He was a small man with twitchy hands and features. His eyes, black as shoe buttons, raked over her, moving slowly down from the top of her reddish hair to the white blouse, frothy with Limerick lace, and over the short green kilt to end on the patent-leather pumps with their huge silver buckles.

"Are you through school yet?"

"I'll graduate from High this June."

"Are you eighteen?"

Stacy nodded. She wouldn't actually be eighteen

until August, but that was what she might as well call herself.

"What are you doing this summer?" His sentences were staccato too, and his fingers plucked nervously at the fancy buttons on his brocade vest.

"Oh—I don't know what I'll do—yet."

"You're just the kind of girl I'm always on the look-out for. Someone with a smile like yours and a voice like yours. You'd go over with a bang. How'd you like a job at my place?"

"You mean singing?"

"Mostly. You might have to do some helping out. I've just opened a nightclub. Something like this place —only we cater to people with big money. We get rushed, you might have to help out with the tables. But when I get a drawing card like you, I go easy on that. Speaking of cards, here's mine. You tuck that away, and when school is out, give me a ring. My place is only thirty miles from Denver."

"That's my mother playing the piano."

"Good—good. Runs in the family, eh. What does Guido pay you for your entertaining tonight?"

"He doesn't pay us—exactly. He slips us each ten dollars when we're leaving."

"Ten bucks! Christamighty, girl, that's peanuts. You'll come out with three times that much in one evening at my place—at least. One of our girls bought a car—that's right, a nifty little secondhand sports car. Paid for it in two months. I run the place. Just ask for Mike when you phone."

Ben was standing beside the piano and motioning her to join them in another song. Stacy had no pocket in her lace-trimmed blouse or short pleated skirt. She slid the card inside her blouse under her bra.

Ben demanded as she joined them, "What did that high-binder with the greasy hair want?"

She could well imagine Ben's questions if she told him the man had offered her a job: "What kind of a joint does he run? What's his name?" Yes, and he'd probably snort, "Doesn't sound on the up-and-up to me. If it was, why wouldn't he talk to Mom about it, instead of waylaying you?"

So she evaded his question. "Oh, he was just saying he liked my song. What are we going to do next?"

Happy hours pass swiftly. Katie Rose's contralto voice was turning husky. Matt, full to the brim with lasagna, topped off with spumoni, kept grumbling, "Can't we go home now?" Miguel said with a contented sigh, "I guess this wraps up another Erin-go-bragh night."

The end of the Erin-go-bragh night came all too soon for Stacy. She liked to sing. She liked applause. And a very good-looking boy with eager eyes had left his party long enough to corner her and ask for her phone number. Under his shock of sun-bleached hair, his face was almost as tanned as Bruce's.

She smiled back at him. "I'm not allowed to give the phone number, but it's Belford on Hubbell Street."

"Belford on Hubbell. I'll engrave that on my heart."

Ben bundled all eight of them into the old Chevvy. Mother, who was to stay on, would come later with the cashier and her husband. On the ride home, Stacy kept telling herself, "A girl is a sap to moon over a fellow. All she needs is to be busy, busy, busy and go, go, go."

She and Jill undressed in their upstairs room together. The card from the man named Mike dropped to the floor when Jill, her back turned, was opening the window.

THE PINK FLAMINGO
AT GREENMONT

Thirty Miles, Thirty Minutes from Denver

*Inspired Gourmet Cuisine • Elegant Decor
And Even More—Nightly Entertainment*

The telephone number was in the corner. Stacy's eyes barely skimmed over it because she didn't want the nosy Jill to see it and ask questions. She opened the shallow top drawer of the dresser, with its jumble of lipsticks, nail files, eye shadow, which students at St. Jude's daren't use, and a compact with a broken mirror. Hastily she slid the white card under the velvet box containing the turquoise necklace.

The man named Mike had scoffed at the ten dollar bill which Guido had pressed into each of their hands as they left. It had always seemed a lot to her before. Imagine getting *three* times that amount for one evening. Imagine a girl making enough in two months to buy a nifty little sports car. Ah, that was a delectable thought. She could fairly feel her own hands on the wheel of her very own car.

All the rest of March, Stacy did go, go, go: school parties, a movie or two with Obie. The boy who had asked for her phone number on St. Patrick's night called her frequently to banter over the phone. She listened to his talk of skiing without admitting that she didn't have the least idea what a slalom or a Christie was.

He drove up in front of her house on a Saturday morning and honked his horn. Ben always put his foot down on either Katie Rose or Stacy running out to the car when a caller honked. "If he wants to see you, he can stir his carcass out and up to the door," he said.

But Ben wasn't home this morning, and Stacy went out. The boy wanted to "line up a date" with her to go skiing at Winter Park that afternoon.

"But I don't ski."

"You don't?" He was as scandalized as though she had said, "I don't take baths."

The skier made only one token call after that to tell her he was going to a collegiate meet in Aspen. She never heard from or thought of him again.

Then there was Claude McIntosh. He had promised to get in touch with her, and he did. But he wasted no time in idle chatter on the phone. "I have to budget my time," he said. He would call to say he didn't have a class Thursday night and ask her to go to the movies. The manager of the shoe department sometimes gave him his symphony tickets for a Sunday afternoon concert when his ailing wife couldn't go. Mother always asked Claude to stay for supper when he brought Stacy home, but he explained that he had studying to do.

"He's such a nice boy," Mother said.

Ben too approved of a young man who hadn't been content to help his father in a small-town grain elevator. He listened to Claude's fund of knowledge about merchandizing. "You know which department in the whole store has the biggest mark-up? Cosmetics. Big profit in furs too, but they don't move so fast."

"Don't you like him, Stacy?" Ben asked hopefully.

"Why, yes, I like him."

One side of him she really did like. That was his small-town, naïve, and easily impressed side. He told of an out-of-town buyer taking him to lunch at an expensive Polynesian restaurant. "Gosh, Stacy, they served gardenias in the women's drinks. And—can you picture it?—the waiter brought damp perfumed napkins for us to wipe our fingers on after the first course."

"Yes, I've heard it's quite something."

"I'll say. While we were there, the buyer got a call, and the waiter plugged the phone in so he could take it right at the table." Then the old strive-and-succeed look replaced the boyish wonder. "You know what I keep thinking? How when I get it made, I'll be getting phone calls like that. I'll have waiters bobbing around to ask if everything is all right."

Stacy told Claire, "Claude budgets his money. You know, so much for tuition, so much for food, so much for gas. And if he runs over the so much for gas, he doesn't use the car. He walks."

"And he carefully counts his change, I'll bet."

"Heavens, yes. Always."

"Is he planning on your sharing his successful future?"

Stacy giggled. "I'm not sure. I think he thinks I should strive harder to improve myself. He gave me a pocket dictionary to help me pronounce words right. He thinks everybody should have a goal in life, and then bend every effort toward it." She added ruefully, "I don't seem to have a goal in life."

Claire had—to be a librarian. This summer she would work in a mountain town where her aunt was in charge of the library's bookmobile. And next fall she would enroll in the librarian course at the university.

"Do you have to fight him off?" Claire asked with interest.

Stacy giggled again. "No, he's not the hot-blooded type. He uses both hands to drive." She couldn't help remembering Bruce and his driving through quiet streets with one hand on the wheel and the other clasping hers.

As though Claire read her thoughts, she scolded, "You're a louse, you know. You don't appreciate the guy's sterling virtues." No answer from Stacy. Claire said bluntly, "I suppose you're still wondering what Bruce was trying to tell you at the Student Union."

"I've about decided," Stacy admitted heavily, "that it wasn't anything. That he was so stoned he didn't know what he was saying—and doesn't even remember seeing me there."

12 ∽

T H E work, the work of putting on a play from scratch! Stacy wanted to be busy, busy, busy, and she couldn't have been more so as the April days ticked by. The two acts were now on paper, and Claire in her spare time was typing out the parts. Stacy helped her, but she was neither as fast nor as accurate a typist as Claire.

The play was to be given on the Thursday and Friday nights before graduation, which would take place on the first Sunday in June. The parts had been assigned by vote of the class. A brown-haired, gray-eyed senior named Linda would play Bernadette the first night and redheaded, slightly green-eyed Stacy would have the role the last. Liesel was given the part of the mother of the sickly baby who was given to fits and who was miraculously cured by the Lady.

No comedy role could be found for Obie. "One thing we won't have to worry about," he said. "And that's holding our lines for laughs."

"Having no stage presence, I'll take over makeup and costumes," Claire volunteered.

The hardest worker of all was Sister Therese. With the scenery crew she painted a backdrop of trees, and spliced wires and bored holes in it with the lighting crew. Looking very un-nunlike in a flowered smock, with her black skirts bunched up to her knees, she clambered up and down ladders. She sawed out odd shapes of fiber board to make the grotto that would house Our Lady.

And what tenacity she had! She located a life-size statue of the Virgin in a garden far out on the edge of town. She took Claire and Stacy with her when she called on the owner. He, a retired lumberman, was most loath to part with it. "We only want to borrow her for awhile," Sister Therese pleaded so insistently that he finally gave in. Well, yes, he further conceded, she *could* put a fresh coat of paint over the blue robe that had faded and weathered in sun, rain, and snow.

After more cajoling, he even consented to let Sister Therese change the sheaf of lilies the Madonna was clasping into a bouquet of roses. "Before we bring her back, I'll change the roses back to lilies," she promised. "And we'll move her with loving care."

The following weekend, she commandeered half the football team to go out with her in Obie's hearse (with the seats removed) to transfer the statue from its garden home to the stage at St. Jude's.

"She had us all take blankets and comforts to wrap it in," Obie told Stacy. "You'd think we were moving a pneumonia patient."

Next came the job of sand-papering the Madonna to smooth down the scabby roughness. Then came Sister Therese's loving strokes of bright blue paint into every fold of her mantle. "I'll work on the roses at night when it's quiet," she said.

Football brawn was again used to hoist the statue into the stage grotto. The auditorium was darkened while the lighting crew tried out the lights. Something was wrong. The Lady looked exactly like what she was —a newly painted statue.

Sister Therese sadly shook her head. "There's no radiance at all—no heavenly glow emanating from her. And my awful roses. I copied a picture out of a seed catalog. They look more like a bunch of radishes."

"Or rhubarb," Obie observed.

Claire said practically, "Maybe if you went to an artists' supply store, you could find some kind of paint that would give off a heavenly glow."

Two days later, Sister Therese was herself all heavenly glow. She stopped Claire and Stacy in the hall. She *had* gone to an artists' supply store, and while there, she had met a young artist. She had told him her problem, and he had scolded her for using a cheap brand of paint. "He says there is a fluorescent kind that glows under artificial light. And he's going to come and help me. I knew St. Jude would guide someone to me."

"Aren't you working St. Jude overtime?" Stacy asked.

"Ah, but he was very close to the Blessed Mother. He would want her to be fittingly garbed."

The next afternoon when the members of the cast

went in the side door of the auditorium, through the wings, and onto the stage, a coatless young man was seated on a high stool in front of the Madonna, putting the finishing touches on the repainted robe.

Even before he turned his head, Stacy knew—for there was no mistaking that shock of tawny hair—that it was Jake who had come to the rescue.

"It's quick-drying paint," Sister Therese said happily. "And just look at *his* roses. He didn't even need a picture from the catalog."

There was no rehearsal that afternoon. Instead, Jake had the cast scatter themselves through the dark auditorium while he and the lighting crew tried out yellow, rose, and lavender lights in various shades and combinations. Stacy was summoned to the stage to kneel in different spots, so that the lighting would be right on her upturned face.

"Look unworldly and edified," Obie coached from the ladder as he shifted a light.

At last Jake was satisfied. "Unkneel yourself, sugar," he said. "This is your lucky day. You get to ride home with me."

Again she settled herself onto the high seat, and waited until he had finished with the rasping gears before she said, "Did you know it was St. Jude who guided you to that paintstore so you'd meet Sister Therese?"

"Do tell. And here I thought I was guided by their sale of Grumbacher paints. How do you know St. Jude gave me a push?"

"Sister Therese told me."

"Ah, that honey babe. What part of heaven did she drop from?"

"I don't know what part of heaven. But I know she came from Milwaukee where her father is a big typhoon in the beer business."

He turned amazed yellowish eyes on her, and snorted out a gusty laugh. "It's *tycoons* that brew up beer and get rich. And *typhoons* that brew up storms, so that people near the ocean have to run for their lives." He snorted again. "Now I know why that guy Bruce can't forget you. You gave him belly laughs, and in that interior decorator house he grew up in, he had sore need of them."

"Says you, he can't forget me," she managed flippantly. "Here, this is our corner."

He stopped in front of the house with such a yank that Stacy rocked in the high seat. "Says I, he can't forget you," he repeated. "Says I, if ever anyone needed someone right now to laugh with, he does."

"There's a word—oh, yes, therapy. Even his mother thought I would be good therapy for him. She wanted me to phone him and sing out, Please, pretty please, lover, come back to me!"

"On you, sugar candy, sarcasm doesn't look so good," he rebuked.

She felt her throat tighten and turned to fumble with the door handle. He tugged at her arm. "Hold everything. I haven't told you why I gave you a ride home. I need someone like you to help me entertain a wardful of patients at the Jewish Hospital. They're all asthmatic and TB kids, and what I aim to do is to make them forget for awhile how hard it is for them to breathe."

He explained that often when he picked up the children's trays, he lingered to draw pictures for them on paper napkins and to make the pictures tell a story. "So I worked up a goofy tale that I can do with stick drawings. It's about a little skunk—I call him Stinkeroo—and his wanting someone to play with him. And how neither the rabbit nor the squirrel, nor this one nor that one, would because—"

"Don't tell me. I can guess."

"You *are* the smart one. Does your grandmother hatch skunks too?"

"No, but you get a good whiff of one every once in a while around Bannon. Where do I come in with little Stinkaroo?"

"You tell the story. While I'm drawing and shifting to different colored pencils, it's hard to do the narrating too. It just dawned on me when I saw you there on St. Jude's stage that you're enough of an actress—"

"Or enough of a ham."

"Sure, sure, but the hammier the better. The kids will love you." He pulled a lumpy wad of note paper out of the bulging pocket of the tweed jacket. "Take this. I think the pages are numbered so you can follow the story. There's one place where the bumblebee sings. You can do that, can't you? It'd sound like a frog croaking if I did."

"Jake, I can chord on a guitar."

"Well, bring it along. Did I tell you it's tomorrow

night? I'll come by for you—about six thirty, because it's lights out for the kids around eight."

"It kind of scares me."

"*Phfff.* There's nothing to be scared of."

She would have liked to have asked him more, but he was in a hurry to get back to the hospital to help on the supper shift.

He opened the car door to call after her, "You read that bit over for a sort of guideline, but you can ad-lib anything you want as we go along. Dress up pretty—the brighter the better."

Inside the house, she dropped down on the piano bench and smoothed out his rumpled pages. Before she had read the story through, she was reaching for her guitar. She experimented in producing a humming sound like a bumblebee. Next she worked on an emphatic *thrum—mm* to accompany each hop the grasshopper made from cabbage to cabbage.

The next evening she donned her brightest dress—a print with tawny yellow flowers and splashes of green leaves. She combed out her long hair and let it hang. After a moment's hesitation, she put on the heavy turquoise necklace. (Aunt Vinia had told her to wear it.)

A corner of white card showed under the box. She had no thought to give it now, but it was nice to know it was there when the time came to call Mike.

She walked down hospital corridors with Jake and stood beside him in the girls' ward. One look around, and her stage fright dissolved into longing to bring smiles to this audience. A few of them were in chairs, but most were propped up on pillows in high cots. The majority of the thirty-some patients were Anglos, but there were also black faces, and the brown ones of Spanish-Americans, and one or two Stacy saw were Indian. Jake had told her they came from all over—Mexico, Hawaii, Alaska. . . .

Two nurses worked to push the beds in position so the occupants could get a good view of the easel and the large pad of drawing paper on it. Another brought a stool for the smudgy shoebox Jake kept his colored pencils in. They were like stubby marking pens, and Stacy helped him to uncap them.

It was magic the way he could start with a clean sheet of paper, and with a few deft strokes, picture a very woeful small skunk with a white stripe, or a squirrel with a bushy tail and a superior look on his face. A few more strokes, and there was a background of trees, flowers, and a rippling brook.

Stacy carried the story along as he drew. She twanged the guitar to accompany each indignant jump of the grasshopper. She sang out the bumblebee's answer to the skunk's plea to play with him, "Go away, Stinkaroo, or I'll sting you."

The story had a happy ending. The small pariah skunk, in utter desolation, hid himself in a bed of mint. And when he emerged, a meadowlark sang out from a tree, "Tweet-tweet-tweet, what smells so sweet? Why, it's you, Stinkeroo. Let me get close to you." In turn, the squirrel, the rabbit, the grasshopper, and the bumblebee all begged him to join their game of hide-and-seek around a hollow log.

While Jake gathered up his equipment, Stacy distributed his drawings among the audience. The first to reach out an eager hand for one was a small Mexican girl. Although her labored breath was like the chug of a washing machine, her smile was so wide it revealed two missing teeth. Stacy squeezed her hand and patted her cheek. That meant handclasps and patted cheeks and good-nights for all, as well as pictures.

They left the children pleased and giggling, but Stacy could not keep back her tears on the way home. "Don't mind me, Jake. I just keep thinking of how you showed them a brook . . . and trees and a cabbage patch . . . and even a boy flying a kite in the background. . . ."

"And you keep thinking how most of those kids won't ever be able to wade in a brook or fly a kite. So do I. But did you notice that they aren't any unhappier than a bunch of young ones playing outdoors on a street corner? Human beings are made of tough gristle."

Stacy wiped away her tears. "I guess I'm like Gran O'Byrne. She says the plucking string to her heart isn't tight enough."

"Don't ever tighten yours, sugar. You were a natural there tonight."

"I like helping them to forget themselves for awhile."

And so had she forgotten herself and her own nagging heartstring had not twinged the entire evening. She mused aloud, "I never once thought of Bruce. I was so busy worrying about Stinkaroo. Jake, everybody

—my family and Claire and Ben's girl Jeanie—thinks I'd be better off if I—if I just went on—and forgot I ever knew him."

"Sure, sure, everybody can tell you how to live your life. But it's your life, sugar. Nobody can live it—with all its hurts and hunks of happiness—for you."

13 ～

$S T A C Y$ first heard the unbelievable,
the earth-shaking news from Claire. On a Tuesday
morning when Stacy was smoothing her wind-blown
hair in front of her locker mirror, Claire grabbed her
arm and whispered urgently, "Come to the library with
me. There's something I can't wait to tell you."

A nun was at the card file in the library when they
entered. Claire, with Stacy in tow, hurried through it
and into the narrow storage room behind, where books
lined the wall.

"You'd never guess in a million years," Claire panted
out. "Old man Seerie took off for Mexico with his ladylove and her two little girls."

Stacy blinked stupidly at her, her lips agape. "You
mean—Bruce's father? Took off for Mexico? I don't believe it. Where did you ever hear such a thing?"

"Straight from the horse's mouth—old Poison Ivy
herself. She came over last night—and if you'd heard
her! I think the reason she couldn't wait to tell us was
because Dad always told her—you know, when she'd

be raving on about dear, wonderful Winifred and all her good works—why, Dad always said he felt sorry for poor downtrodden Mr. Seerie with a wife that wielded a gavel instead of an egg beater. So I guess old Englemann couldn't wait to tell Dad what a lowdown cur Seerie turned out to be."

Stacy repeated, "I can't believe it—not Mr. Seerie." She had an instant's picture of the dapper, self-contained, smooth-tongued lawyer with his watchful eyes and thin lips. He was the last man in the world she could imagine kicking over the traces and leaving that split-level house of his. She asked in a stunned voice, "Did you say with a ladylove?"

"And her two little girls. They're not even in school yet. Englemann says she's young enough to be his daughter. She said she's a scheming young divorcée that set her cap for Seerie because he has money. She says she worked on his sympathy because she was crippled up with her torn ligament, and—"

"Oh, that one," Stacy breathed.

"Englemann feels so sorry for Mrs. Seerie she hasn't slept for two nights."

"I feel sorry for Bruce." She felt a sudden longing to reach out to him and say I'm so sorry.

The bell rang then, and Claire had only time to add, "If I hear any more details, I'll let you know."

The only details she had to relay to Stacy during the next days were of her neighbor's growing sympathy for the wronged wife and her irate comments on the wrongdoer or doers. "She says Seerie and that woman are living in sin in Mexico. She says dear wonderful

Winifred is the bravest soul she has ever known. That she hasn't canceled even one of her club meetings in spite of the terrible humiliation she's suffering."

On Saturday, which was the last Saturday in April and a day of gray beclouded skies, Stacy heard a somewhat different version of the cataclysmic affair than that given by Claire's neighbor.

Beany Buell, née Malone, for whom Stacy often baby-sat, phoned her in mid-afternoon. In a voice quite unlike her usual lilting one, Beany asked Stacy if she were free that afternoon.

"You don't sound like you, Mrs. Buell."

"I don't feel like myself either. My right jaw is swollen up like a basketball. It's one of my wisdom teeth. It started acting up last night, and I've been putting on hot compresses till one side of my face is all but parboiled. I've just got to get down to the dentist, but I have Mister and Mary Liz on my hands."

"You want me to stay with the children?"

"I'd like you to drive me and them downtown first." Her husband, Beany explained, was at his law office finishing up some work. But he had tracked down their dentist, and the dentist had agreed to take Beany at three if she came to his office. "I can manage to drive myself and the children to your house, Stacy. Then if you can drive us all downtown, and drop me at the dentist's—"

"How will you get home?"

"Carl will bring me. He's to meet me at the dentist's."

"Sure, I'll be glad to do it. I'll be watching for you."

Stacy was ready, and she ran out the minute the Buell car stopped. Beany slid out of the driver's seat, and said around the man's handkerchief she was holding to her puffy jaw, "Just take it slow, honey, till you get the feel of the car. And you two keep quiet in the back, do you hear? Get back on the seat, Mary Liz. Better hold on to her, Mister."

The small boy helped the bouncy toddler onto the seat, and asked with grave concern, "Does it still hurt so bad, Mother?"

"Not so bad," she told him, and in a wry aside to Stacy, "Not as bad as it's going to when the dentist does whatever he decides to do."

"I had a wisdom tooth pulled," Stacy cheered her. "And it didn't hurt for very long."

"I'll be glad to part company with it," Beany mumbled.

Downtown traffic was not so worrisome on Saturday afternoon when most offices were closed. Without difficulty, Stacy reached the building where the dentist was waiting for his patient. She double-parked while Beany climbed out and gave hurried injunctions to the backseat passengers, "Don't you two make any trouble for Stacy when she's driving home. And take your naps without any arguing."

Stacy further insured their making her no trouble by promising them that if they both sat as quiet as little mice in the back seat, she would sing each of them a song before they took their naps.

"You mean a song for eachbody?" Mister queried.

"You bet. A song for eachbody, and whichever one eachbody chooses."

Back in the ranch-style house on Laurel Lane while Mister deliberated on his choice, she sang "Jack and Jill" to Mary Liz.

Mister finally decided on "I Have No Use for the Women," so Stacy sang lustily about the honest young cowboy who went astray because of a girl named Lou:

> Oh, I have no use for the women,
> A true one can never be found.

When Carlton Buell's car drove into the graveled driveway an hour later, both children were still fast asleep. Stacy hurried to put on the teakettle. Carlton ushered in a wan-looking Beany who was now holding a wad of blood-spotted tissue over her mouth.

"Ah, he pulled it," Stacy commiserated in a low voice because of the sleeping children. "I'll have some hot tea for you in a minute."

Beany could only nod. She hurried to the bathroom from which she emerged with a fresh wad of tissue. Her voice came muffled through it as she dropped down on a kitchen stool, "Stacy, Jeanie Kincaid tells me you don't go with Bruce Seerie anymore. But weren't you just as dumfounded as everyone else to hear about his father?"

Stacy tilted the teakettle and poured boiling water over the tea leaves. "I still can't believe it."

There was that old rat-a-tat of her heart again, and the rush of sympathy as she wondered how Bruce was taking it. She longed to hear more about him. "All I know is what a friend of Mrs. Seerie's told Claire's family. She's a schoolteacher named Englemann who lives next door to Claire. She thinks that Mr. Seerie is a lowdown cur and that Mrs. Seerie is a saint. Do you folks know anything about it?"

Carlton reached for a cup from the cupboard. "Here, Beany, drink some tea and never mind the gossip."

Beany made another sortie to the bathroom for another fresh handful of tissue. Returning, she left a corner of her mouth uncovered long enough to say, "I know one thing, Stacy. When I heard about Seerie walking out on his club-woman wife, I almost resigned from the two clubs I belong to so my husband wouldn't do likewise."

"Listen to the woman!" her husband said. He shook two aspirins out of the bottle and handed them to her. "Take these, drink your tea, and then I'll bundle you off to bed before I drive Stacy home."

Between somewhat painful sips of tea, Beany went on, "You should hear Connie's version of it. Connie is Carl's secretary, and she knows Louise. Louise is the 'other woman,' and Connie says she's not a hussy at all. She says it's a case of true love, and it's beautiful to see how much Seerie and Louise mean to each other."

"It's never beautiful when the fellow walks out on his wife and child," Carlton said shortly.

Beany was looking so spent and shaky that he didn't let her finish her tea but guided her down the hall and tucked her into bed. Stacy put on her green St. Jude blazer, and went out with Carlton through a fine mist to his car.

But she still wanted to know more about the Seerie affair. She said as they drove down Laurel Lane, "This Englemann woman—Claire calls her Poison Ivy—said that the girl was a young divorcée and that she had made a play for Mr. Seerie because he had money and she wanted someone to support her and her two little girls."

"She's wrong on both counts. She's a young widow, and she didn't make a play for him. The whole thing started when Louise fell at the Christmas party in Seerie's office." Carlton told again of the young mother's anxiety to leave early so as to Christmas-shop for her children, of the man grabbing her arm and of her fall, and of Mr. Seerie taking her to the hospital for X rays.

"Yes, Bruce told me about his father being way late getting home to their Christmas Eve dinner. Bruce said he even hustled up some food for the two hungry little girls and Louise."

Carlton had more to add to that. "Louise had been helping in his office with inventory. She couldn't take the bus with her leg in the cast, so Seerie picked her up every morning and took her home in the evening."

"I never liked him," Stacy said. "I can't even imagine his doing anything nice for anyone."

"I've never cared for Seerie either. He's too sharp, too devious, too grasping for my taste. But to give the devil his due— Well, what with all Mrs. Seerie's outside activities, the poor fellow was just the provider, the writer-out of checks at home. Connie said he told his secretary that when he brought Louise home in the evening, the little girls would be glued to the window watching for him. And they'd race out and throw their arms around him." He gave a wry laugh. "I don't imagine he had anyone racing out or throwing their arms around him at home."

They were held up before making the turn onto College Boulevard by a solid stream of traffic. "The basketball game must have just let out," he said. "I wonder how our team came out with Wyoming."

But Stacy wasn't interested in basketball games right then. "This Englemann woman feels so sorry for Mrs. Seerie that she can't sleep. She says—"

He interrupted with a barking grunt. "I wouldn't lose any sleep over Mrs. Seerie. I was talking to Seerie's law partner. Don't ever think, Stacy, that men don't gossip as much as women. And he tells me he never knew a woman as adamant or vindictive or as mercenary as Mrs. Seerie. Seerie wants a divorce so he can marry this girl, and his partner—Gibbons is his name—says Mrs. Seerie will bleed him dry financially before she gives it to him."

"Did Mr. Seerie's law partner say anything about Bruce?"

"Yes, he did. Before he left, Bruce's father set up a trust fund for Bruce's education. The sort that would let Bruce draw so much each month. When Gibbons had Bruce come down to arrange for the payments, his mother arrived with him. Bruce refused to accept the

fund his father left. He said he didn't want any conscience money. That infuriated Mrs. Seerie, and she
turned on Bruce. Gibbons said she made a sickening
scene in the office, just lacing down the kid—"

Oh, poor Bruce.

"So Gibbons said he phoned the Seerie residence the
next day, hoping he could get hold of Bruce. He
wanted to talk to him *alone* and see if he could reason
with him. But his mother answered—"

At last, there was a break in the heavy line of traffic
and Carlton made a swift turn onto the Boulevard.

"What did Bruce's mother say?" Stacy prodded.

"She said that Bruce had left home and couldn't be
reached by phone. That he'd gone to stay with a very
disreputable friend."

"I'll bet it's Jake," Stacy murmured. "But he isn't disreputable."

"Gibbons tells me Bruce is in a bad way. He's quit
school. He's bitter at his father, and even more bitter at
his mother for driving such a merciless bargain and—"

Stacy cried out suddenly, "Mr. Buell, let me out on
the next corner. Right there by Schmitty's place."

He slowed down, giving her a surprised look. "Why
at Schmitty's in this drizzle?"

"I want to see Bruce. And Jake's place is just down
the street a ways from Schmitty's."

"I thought you and Bruce had broken up."

"We did. But—but—" *But her only thought was to
see him now and say, "Bruce, I'm so sorry about all
this."* She suddenly remembered a sodden Bruce and
his clutching her wrist and his incoherent babbling,

"There's something I want to tell you." She wished now that in spite of Claude's sticking so close, in spite of the crowd around them, she had somehow been able to listen to him.

"Stacy, sometimes a bear would rather nurse his wounds in private. Maybe you'd better hold off awhile —maybe send him a note."

"No, no. I just want to see him."

"Okay. Show me where he lives, and I'll drop you off."

She directed him to turn off the Boulevard at Schmitty's corner. She pointed out the house with the red of the bricks showing through the coat of white paint.

"Why don't I go in with you, Stacy?"

"No. No, I'd rather you didn't, Mr. Buell."

"Then I'll wait out here so you won't have to walk home in the drizzle."

"Oh, no, no. I mean—it's not far from home—and I like to walk in the rain." It was a feeble excuse, but Carlton Buell didn't press the point. He only said, "I almost forget to pay the baby-sitter," and took three dollar bills out of his wallet.

"That's way *way* too much. I was only there about two hours."

"As long as plumbers get extra for emergency calls on Saturday, baby-sitters ought to rate too," he said and shoved the bills into her pocket. He let her out and drove on.

Her eyes probed the cars in the vacant lot. Jake's red station wagon was not there. Neither was the copper-colored car which she had seen last on that January day when Bruce drove away from the Belford house on the corner.

The narrow walk Stacy took around the house was bordered by wet spirea bushes. Under an outdoor table in the backyard, a big yellow cat was crouched. It watched her out of unconcerned amber eyes.

The steps leading to the basement must have also once been painted white, but the paint in the middle of them had all worn off. She knocked at the solid basement door. No one opened it for her, and she rapped louder. She heard a voice call out something, but she couldn't tell what it said.

She pushed open the door and took a faltering step inside.

14 ❧

W$_{HEN}$ Stacy stepped inside the basement room, the loud sound of a voice on TV assailed her ears, and simultaneously the unaired stuffiness of the room assailed her nose. The sour heaviness of the air—a mingling of oil paints, stale cigarettes, and the brown acrid smell of a coffeepot that has boiled dry—was all the more noticeable after the misty freshness outside.

She stood there a moment, her eyes trying to accustom themselves to the dim murkiness broken only by the shifting light from the TV screen. On it, as a prelude to a commercial, two children frolicked on a beach with a collie dog.

Her eyes moved to the big hump of an upholstered chair. It had been covered by a faded Indian blanket that was now pulled out of place, so that the gray-white stuffing it was meant to cover showed. Then she noticed the pair of feet clad in dirty white unlaced tennis shoes dangling over the bulging chair arm. They belonged to a figure slumped sidewise in the chair.

It was Bruce. And yet not Bruce. Not the Bruce who

had knocked on the Belford door on Christmas day in his new handknit sweater, his face glowing from the cold. This Bruce wore a grimy gray sweatshirt, and his face was sallow and slack.

The old Bruce would have got to his feet the moment a girl came into the room. He would have instantly turned off the TV, which was now blaring about a detergent that laughed at muddy stains. But this new Bruce only looked at her out of blank hostile eyes.

She said inanely, "Bruce, it's me—Stacy."

"So I see. I thought it was old pussyfoot from Dad's office. What do you want?"

"I just wanted to tell you that— I mean, I'm sorry about . . . about all the trouble. . . ."

He gave a short ugly snort of laughter. "That's nice of you to come with your condolences. I can do without them." He moved his eyes back to the TV screen. It now showed a golf course where a player and caddy moved ahead of a group of spectators.

Stacy ventured again, "I didn't see Jake's red station wagon outside."

"He's made for the hills, maybe to paint, maybe to pound a few nails into his falling-down cabin." He kept his eyes fixed on the screen and the golfer who swung at the ball. "Nice drive," he muttered to himself as though she weren't there.

"I didn't see your car either."

"The carrot, you mean. No, when the donkey couldn't be led by it, it was taken back."

"I thought—I mean, you said you were going to help

Jake rebuild his house up there. You said Jake wasn't much good at—at putting in windows."

"Go ahead, say it. Say I'd be better off up there in good clean mountain air than sitting here in this messy dump. If you don't, you'll be my first caller that hasn't."

He made a groping motion toward the floor and picked up a can of tobacco. From his rumpled jeans he drew out a package of cigarette papers. *Imagine Bruce rolling his own.* The cigarette came out very thin and wispy at each end and lumpy in the middle. He lit it, but it didn't burn well. He dropped it on the floor and swung his feet around to grind it out in the faded dirty rug. *Imagine Bruce doing that.*

"I can't ask you if you're hungry," he said mockingly, "because there's nothing to eat in this hole in the wall. I looked myself. Nothing but a can of water chestnuts that Jake—or even Allegra—can't figure out what to do with."

"I'm not hungry."

"I was. But not now. Not after all the uninvited visitors. First the coach. Mom put him up to it, of course. He gave me his Boy Scout pep talk. He called this cozy little apartment of Jake's a rabbit hutch. But Allegra will be in any day, and she'll muck it out for us. Now there's a gal for you. And then old pussyfoot who used to be Dad's partner came. More of the same. Oh, yes, this is my at-home day. Even Aunt Vinia took it upon herself to come. She went the coach one better—she called this place a hog wallow. She wanted to grab me out of it and put me in her front room upstairs where I used to stay when I was a kid."

"You know, Bruce, that was one of the happiest times of my life. That day we went to see Aunt Vinia, I mean. Remember? And you took her the timer, and she—"

"Ancient history," he said gruffly.

A long pause while his eyes remained riveted on the golf meet on TV.

"Bruce, that night at the Student Union. When you said you wanted to tell me something— I mean, I'm sorry things were the way they were—"

Dear heaven, she shouldn't have said that. She could see by the look on his face that he was remembering that scene he had had to retreat from in ignominy.

He said brutally, "I don't remember ever wanting to tell you anything."

Another long silence except for a TV commercial about a brand of coffee with a built-in lift and smile. She stood, her purse over her arm, wondering what to say next. With the forefinger of her right hand—and not knowing she was doing it—she nervously tolled off over and over the fingers on her left hand.

"Stop counting your fingers," he shouted. "You've got four of them and one thumb on each hand, in case you didn't know. And stop saying you're sorry. What are you sorry about? Because Mom couldn't call this particular meeting to order? Because the old boy found someone that thought *he* was more important than saving old landmarks? Or because he now has two sweet little cherubs to drool over?"

"Please, Bruce. I hate to see you so bitter about it."

"Me bitter?" Again that ugly snort of laughter. "I'm not bitter. That's why I left home. Because I had to listen to her tirades. Pure wormwood. And because I wouldn't join in the chorus. So the old boy washed me out of his life. So I wiped my poor done-wrong-by mother out of mine. Because her joy in wringing him dry turned my stomach. I never knew how wonderful orphans had it."

He groped again for the can of tobacco, again shook some into the thin rectangle of paper. He did a worse job than before in rolling it. This one spilled out at both ends. The match folder he opened was empty, and he hurled it across the room. He pulled himself out of the chair with a mutter about finding some matches. The mutter was all but drowned out by loud cheering from the TV. If only he would—or if only she dared—turn it off!

He pushed past her into a small box of a room adjoining the larger one. He said as though it were of consequence, "This was the coal room before they made it into a kitchen."

Her eyes followed him. She could see the dirty clutter of greasy skillet and egg shells on the stove. Yes, the coffee pot *had* boiled over first before it boiled dry; there were blackish-brown stains running down its aluminum sides.

He squatted down and pulled out the lower drawer in a cupboard. Stacy could see the assorted debris of can opener, mussed paper napkins, jar tops, fly swatter, and tangled string that he clattered through in his search for matches.

He turned his head and demanded unexpectedly, "What did you say you came for?"

She stepped closer to him. "I came because I realized what an awful shock your father's leaving was—and I just wanted to—"

"Yes, yes, now I remember. You came to offer sympathy over the great shock of my father's sky-hooting off to Mexico with the light of his life and those cuddly little kids of hers." He stood upright. "Well, let me tell you something. That wasn't the shock you seem to think it was. The shock came a lot earlier. In February when Mom was back in Washington telling the Woman Voters like it is. In February when the Shrine Circus was held out at the coliseum."

"The Shrine Circus," she repeated dazedly.

"Yes, the Shrine Circus. Because it so happened that Mr. Seerie's son"—he went on in an affected voice but with bleak eyes—"was driving home from a freshman game in Boulder. That was when Seerie junior was the coach's fair-haired boy. And it so happened that he got caught in the traffic jam as the circus was letting out. So he had to sit there in what a girl once called his mother's perfumed car—no, I believe carrot was the latest word for it. He sat there while the policeman held up the cars to give the pedestrians a chance to cross the street. And that's when he saw the happy family. They passed right smack-dab in front of him. The man was guiding the woman in her walking cast with one loving arm and carrying one of the little tots in the other. The other little girl held tight to his coat-tail. If the dope behind the wheel hadn't recognized the Brooks Brothers suit and the tie he had given him for Christmas—"

"Oh, Bruce. That's terrible. Didn't he see you?"

"See *me?* Are you kidding? He had eyes only for his dear ones and getting them safely across the street." Quite devoid of his smart-aleck air, he added slowly, "Stacy, I don't ever remember him carrying *me* across a street with such—such tenderness. . . .

His face seemed to crumple before her eyes. She took a quick step closer to him and reached out her hand.

He knocked it aside with sudden vehemence. Just as swiftly he turned back to the open drawer and bent low to rattle through its contents again. With his back to her and his head all but thrust into the drawer, he bellowed out, "Can't you take a hint for godssake! I know where you live. When I crave your sympathy, I'll come crawling down there." Still rattling loudly in the drawer, he yelled with even fiercer anger, "Nobody asked you to come here. I stayed home to watch a golf match on TV. All I want is to be left alone. Get out. Get out. Get out and stay out."

Stacy got out. She neither knew nor cared whether she closed the heavy door behind her or not. Unsteadily she climbed the once-white steps, that led back to the fresh air of the misty wet world.

Nothing seemed real. The boy who had bellowed at her to get out and stay out wasn't Bruce. He was a stranger who resembled him. The mocking voice, the unsocked feet in dirty tennis shoes, didn't belong to Bruce but to that stranger.

15 ～

A *G A I N* Stacy followed the walkway around the house. This time she was generously sprayed by the wet spirea bushes. Suddenly the narrow path was blocked by the oncoming figure of a girl. When Stacy raised her eyes, she saw that it was Allegra with her wet bangs plastered down on her forehead and her wide glowing smile.

"It's you, Stacy. Gee, I'm glad to see you."

Stacy wanted to say "I'm glad to see you too, Allegra," but she was afraid to open her mouth for fear she would cry.

Allegra was still wearing the short bunchy belted coat Stacy had first seen her in, but the leopard slacks had now been replaced by ones of well-worn magenta plaid. She looked away from Stacy at the cars parked in the lot by the side of the house. "I don't see Jake's station wagon. I guess he isn't home yet."

Stacy shook her head.

Allegra looked at her more closely. "Bruce is, I suppose, and in one of his lousy moods. Near suicidal, Jake calls them."

Stacy nodded this time.

"You didn't see any sign of anything to eat down there, did you?"

Stacy shook her head. And then for fear she might seem unsociable, she managed, "Not even coffee. The pot had boiled over—and dry. There's just a can of water chestnuts, he said."

"Oh, yes, those water chestnuts. What can you do with the fool things? I could sure go for a cup of coffee," Allegra said with a shiver. "I walked all the way over here, and all I've had to eat all day is an apple."

Stacy's thoughts lifted from her own bruised bewilderment. "Schmitty's is right there on the corner. We could go there for coffee."

"I haven't got any money."

"I have."

"Oh, good." Allegra laughed in childlike delight. "And if you don't take cream in your coffee, don't tell Schmitty and I'll put yours in mine. Come on."

She turned and hurried back around the house and past the parking lot with Stacy following. She had a farm girl's lumbering walk as though she were used to walking over rough fields. She pushed open the door of the lunchroom and held it for Stacy. "I sure will be glad to sit down where it's warm."

On school days Schmitty's popular hangout was always crowded and noisy. But this late Saturday afternoon there were many empty tables, and the juke box for once was silent.

Allegra lost no time in turning her eager smile on the rotund aproned proprietor who was gathering up empty plates at the table next to theirs. "Two coffees and trimmings, Schmitty."

The two cups of coffee were set before them. Allegra promptly emptied the miniature pitcher of cream and the packet of sugar into hers, and gave the coffee a quick stir before taking a gulp. "Now I've got room for your cream." She reached for Stacy's with a "sure you don't mind?" poured it in too, and shook in the other packet of sugar. "Umm-mm, it's so good," she said after another grateful gulp.

She slid off the tan coat. Under it was the crocheted sweater with the loose mesh she had worn to the St. Patrick's Day party at the Student Union. It had stretched even more in wearing and washing, so that she had to keep tugging it up on first one shoulder and then the other.

Katie Rose was always scolding Mother for the slap-dash combination of clothes she wore, but even she, Stacy thought, would never wear a wide-necked lacy sweater with tight plaid slacks under the dressy old-fashioned coat. And yet as Stacy looked at the uneven bangs and beatific smile, her heart went out to her.

She noticed Allegra's nostrils twitching hungrily as Schmitty carried a corned-beef sandwich past their table. "Wouldn't you like a sandwich, Allegra?"

"Gosh, hon, they cost eighty-five cents. That's too much for you to—"

"Oh, no. I'm loaded. I just got paid double for baby-sitting." She caught Schmitty's eye as he started back to the counter and told him to bring Allegra a sandwich too. Seeing the nearly empty coffee cup in front of her, Stacy added, "And another coffee."

"I'm out of a job," Allegra stated ruefully.

"Is that the job you lost because you fed Jake when he was hungry?"

Allegra laughed. "No, that was at the Purple Cow. That old tightwad boss. Then I got the one at Grandpa's Pancake House. Only I'm so dumb. I gave that one up because a girl told me about another job she was sure I could get. Where all the tips were folding money, she said. It was in a little burg—My gracious, I can't remember the name of the place. I'd be working there now only the police closed it down."

"They did. What for?"

"I don't know. This friend called me long distance from her brother's, and she couldn't talk a lot, you know. But it'll be opening up again any day. That's what this girl said."

She looked across at Stacy and the almost full cup of coffee in front of her. "Oh, lambie, don't just sit there hugging your hurt. Wasn't Bruce nice to you?"

"He yelled at me to get out. To get out and stay out."

"You should never have come. As Jake says, it's better just to let him stew in his own juice."

"I—I only wanted to tell him I was sorry—about things. He—said—he didn't want my sympa—thy—" She stopped at that because of the lump in her throat.

Allegra reached a hand across the table to her. "Don't take his being so hateful to heart. Jake says he's the chicken fresh out of the egg. He says Bruce was so used to the shell around him that now he doesn't know which way to turn. You know how Jake talks."

"He didn't seem like Bruce at all. I never thought I'd hear him talk about his family—especially his mother —the way he did."

"He's just discovered what an old witch she is. Gosh, was she ever insulting to me when I phoned Bruce once. And I made her madder because I kept laughing. Craziest thing—lots of times when I'm happy I cry, but when something or somebody hurts me, I laugh like a hyena."

"She hurt me too. Only I didn't laugh." Stacy huddled back in her misery.

Allegra's concerned eyes looked at her over the cup of coffee she was draining to the last drop. "Are you in love with Bruce?" she asked with childlike candor.

"I . . . don't . . . know."

Was it love when you felt utter happiness just sitting beside someone? Was it love when that guttural shout of "nobody asked you to come" still clanged in your ears?

"I'm in love," Allegra said with that same disarming honesty.

"With Jake?"

"Oh, no. Jake's just a swell friend. He's someone I can always turn to. No, his name is Robbie. He went to school with me, and then he worked in the freezer plant at Opal—that's where I lived. Then he had to go into the army"—her face became suddenly luminous— "and he kissed me good-bye. It was the first time he ever had. Grandpa saw us, and he slapped me like everything when I came in. And he sent me to bed without any supper and made me read parts in the Bible—you know, about the sins of the flesh. But I didn't mind—not a bit." Her remembering smile was undimmed.

"Did you live with your grandpa? Are your folks dead?"

"No, Mammy still lives down there. She's married again. But her second husband has a son who is a big lubberly lout. One night I was alone there, when Mammy and her husband had gone off on a trip, and he tried to get into my bedroom. The door was bolted—not a very strong bolt though—and I saw he was shoving the door so hard that it soon wouldn't hold. So I quickly climbed out the window onto the roof of the back porch. And then I sort of hung onto the edge and dropped to the ground—"

"From the roof of the porch? Didn't you hurt yourself?"

"Just a sprained ankle. I hid in the alfalfa stack for awhile, and then I found a saddle blanket in the barn, and I wrapped it around me over my nightgown and went to Grandpa's. That's how I came to live with him," she finished in simple explanation.

"Didn't your ankle hurt? How far was it?"

"It was about three miles, cutting across the fields. My ankle hurt a little at first, and then it got so cold I couldn't feel anything. It was winter, you know." This too she told with no more resentment than if she said, "I had oatmeal for breakfast."

"But didn't you tell anybody about that lout? He ought to have been arrested."

"He wouldn't have been." Her shrug was one of acceptance. "There'd just have been a lot of tongue-wagging. That's the way people are in a little town."

"I should think your grandpa would have wondered about your showing up that way. I mean, in your nightgown with a blanket over it."

"You'd have laughed about that, Stacy. Grandpa is sort of batty about religion. He thinks the Lord listens to him and looks after him. I guess he'd been telling Him that he needed someone to come and stay with him because he was so crippled up he couldn't milk his cow. So he thought the Lord sent me—saddle blanket and all."

Stacy could only stare at her in wonder. Jake had said Allegra was one of the pure in heart, that she could go through the slime and filth of the world and come out untouched. And Bruce had said, "There's a gal for you."

Schmitty set another cup of coffee in front of her and a sandwich with its inch-thick filling of corned beef. After two bites of it, Allegra added fondly, "Grandpa was good to me in his way. I didn't mind his making me read the Bible every night."

"Maybe if your mother knew you were out of a job, she could—well, help you out, couldn't she?"

"Maybe. But she's got troubles of her own since she got married again. She was always man-crazy." Again that gentle shrug of acceptance. "If you don't expect anybody to be better than they are—or different than they are—then you aren't ever disappointed." She added, apropos of nothing, "Robbie has the bluest blue eyes you ever saw."

Stacy asked earnestly, "How do you know for sure you're in love with him?"

Allegra held a potato chip poised to say, "When I'm happy about something I just wish I could tell him about it. And when everything just goes out from under, I want to reach out for his hand. Whenever I'm hungry and cold, I pray—only I'm not as good a prayer as Grandpa—that he's warm and has a full stomach."

That was the way I felt for the Bruce I was so sure was rugged and manly. It was that Bruce I always reached out for. And it was the mama's boy I fought with and said hateful things to when—

"Robbie's in Vietnam now."

Again Stacy was roused from her own woe. "Do you write back and forth?"

"Oh, my, yes. You ought to see the postcards I've got. But I haven't heard from him for awhile. Maybe he sent me cards or maybe a letter that I didn't get because lately I've moved around a lot."

By now every crust and crumb of the sandwich, every potato chip and slice of dill pickle—even the wisp of lettuce—had vanished. Allegra sighed contentedly. "Thank you, Stacy, thanks a thousand. Now I'll be able to hoof it down to Grandpa's Pancake place and see if they can use some help. They may be kind of uppity because I told them about the super job I was going to get."

They walked out together into the misty dusk and down the Boulevard. At the corner by Downey's Drug their ways divided. Stacy pressed the two dollars she took from her billfold into Allegra's reluctant hand. "No, take it. Please take it. Because—oh, Allegra, I don't want you to be hungry again—not ever again."

Allegra threw her arms around her. "Nobody ever said that to me before—nobody—" She was crying. All unbidden, Stacy's own held-back tears came.

The two stood there together on the corner, the drizzle and their tears wetting their cheeks while each one patted the other's back and choked out, "Don't cry. Don't cry now. . . ."

16 ～

S I S T E R Therese's hands shook as she arranged the gray chiffon scarf to cover Stacy's red hair. Everyone else backstage on this Friday night, which was the second and final performance of "Bernadette," was jittery too. The auditorium was rapidly filling with students, parents, and friends, and the reason for Sister Therese's extra nervousness was that the bishop himself was seated in the third row.

The girl who had played Bernadette the night before had left her brown hair uncovered. But Sister Therese had carefully read every description in Franz Werfel's book and could find no reference to the little peasant girl's having any red in her hair. It was Stacy's mother who had produced the scarf. Digging deep in her "dirt-cheap" chest, she had extracted the rumpled and generous square of gray chiffon with the price tag, ten cents, still on it.

First Claire, who was in charge of makeup and costumes, had folded the square into a triangle and tied it under Stacy's chin. No, oh, no, Sister Therese had said. She had tried folding it into a rectangle and knotting it first under Stacy's chin and then under her ear. That hadn't been right either—too ungraceful and bulky. Now her shaky fingers draped it over Stacy's hair with an end over each shoulder.

But she was afraid it would slide off. Her robes flying, she raced down the hall to the office for transparent Scotch tape to fix the scarf firmly to Stacy's forehead. In the process a few hairs were caught under it, and they pulled each time Stacy turned her head.

"Make her look more sallow," the nun advised Claire as she backed off and surveyed her. "She still looks too healthy. Bernadette was sickly, remember."

Besides the scarf, Stacy wore a peasant smock and wooden shoes. And between them she had on what she called a "galumpish" skirt, meaning that it was made of heavy wool and ended halfway between knee and ankle. It was an old one that had belonged to the well-fleshed Liz, with the waistband taken in by safety pins.

Liesel, playing the mother of a hopelessly sick child, wanted to wear an orange-colored smock, but Sister Therese had firmly vetoed that. "No, indeed, child. We can't have bright colors on the stage detracting from the softer shades of Our Lady in the grotto."

The growing flutter under Stacy's ribs was more than stage fright and more than the fact that his Excellency, the bishop, sat in the third row. For Sister Therese had mentioned that she had given Jake complimentary tickets to the show in return for his labor and skill. "He said he'd like three so he could bring two friends."

Surely that could only mean that Allegra and Bruce would be sitting beside him in the audience. *And just how should a girl act toward a boy who had slapped down her hand when she stretched it out to him in sympathy? Or, more important, just how would the boy act toward her?*

Claire smoothed a yellow ocher makeup over the red flush in Stacy's cheeks. "Is your strive-and-succeed hero coming to see you play?"

"He's taking a final this evening. He'll come when he's finished."

"That figures," Claire grunted.

The school orchestra struck up boldly. The curtains parted. As usual, Stacy's stage fright lasted for only a panicky moment as she walked over the gritty earth of the stage. "Just turn yourself into the person you're playing," Grandda, veteran of the theater, always said. So she turned herself into the peasant girl who gathered driftwood for fuel and who stopped to rest on a fallen log while her sister and school friend foraged on ahead. She became the awestruck girl who suddenly saw the Lady bathed in radiance standing in the filthy rock cavern.

The First Act curtain went down to appreciative applause.

Scene one of the second act included everyone in the large cast. Townspeople, relatives, curiosity seekers, politicians, all seeking somehow to benefit themselves from Bernadette's vision. And in between all the badgering and bickering, there were the miracles of healing.

In scene two an older Bernadette, pledged now to convent life, came for the last time to say farewell to the Lady who had brought her an abiding faith within, in spite of the hectoring and scoffing from without. Bernadette knelt in the old spot, hoping for a final glimpse of the Lady, a final fortifying of her soul.

A strange thing happened to Stacy as she knelt there, and in answer to her entreaty, the glow and radiance lighted up the grotto and the Madonna with her armful of roses again appeared. This was the cue for the orchestra to play softly "Ave Maria."

Stacy knew, of course, that the figure had been carted from the lumberman's garden and given a coat of fluorescent paint. She knew that backstage boy electricians were pushing switches to produce the suffusion of heavenly light. But for a flickering instant or two the scene was as real to her as it had been to little Bernadette. She no longer felt the tape pulling her forehead or the gravelly grit pressing into her knees.

Instead she felt herself transfigured with the same surge of love and compassion she had felt on Christmas morning among the poinsettias. She even had a second of vowing that she wouldn't be so snappish to Jill or so resentful of Ben's bossing, and a flash of understanding and empathy with the bear of a Bruce wanting to lick his wounds in private. Like Bernadette, she knew a strengthening and peace of soul.

The thundering applause and swish of the closing curtains roused her. She got up slowly and dislodged the sharp granules pressing into her knees.

Yet some of the peace remained while she took curtain calls with the cast, and her eyes swiftly traveled over the audience trying to locate Jake and his friends. *I won't keep saying I'm sorry this time. I'll just get across to him that I'd like to help.*

She bowed and smiled her thanks for the two bouquets the girl ushers came rushing up the aisle with, and the rat-a-tat pounded under her smock. *Maybe one is from him.*

Neither one was. The red roses were from the football team for which as cheerleader she yelled herself hoarse on Saturday afternoons. The pink carnations bore a card: "To my best girl. I'll come for you after the exam."

Her wondrous peace and love began to ebb. She unstuck the tape from her forehead, conscious once again of its pulling.

The crowd was directed from the auditorium to the gym where the junior class was serving coffee, soft drinks, and cookies. An excited Sister Therese enjoined the cast not to take off their costumes yet. A photographer from the morning *Call* was waiting in the gym to take pictures.

Stacy posed first with the cast and then alone, holding the football team's roses. She received congratulations. She listened to Sister Therese telling her that the bishop had said that her, Stacy's, spiritual quality was quite manifest and edifying to the audience. Linda, the

Bernadette of the previous evening, overheard the remark and snorted. "I might've looked spiritual, too, if gravel hadn't been digging into my legs. Sister Therese and her truckload of dirt!"

All the while Stacy talked and shook hands, her eyes sifted through the crowd. Ah, there was Jake. And here came Allegra, hurrying in her ungainly way from the refreshment table to throw her arms around Stacy and to say around the mouthful of cookies she was crunching, "It was beautiful, Stacy—and just as real as real— and I'm so glad Jake brought me. That place I was telling you about that the police closed—it's opening up next week."

"Did just you—just you and Jake come?"

"We wanted Bruce to. Jake told him he had a ticket for him. We told him you were the lead. But he just took off without—"

Jake pushed up then. "I can't bear to see you looking like a case of yellow jaundice, sugar. Here, let me—" He used his paper napkin to wipe off her makeup. "Hah, there're the rosy cheeks showing through." He finished Allegra's sentence, "Yeh, buster took off without even saying where he was headed for."

"I don't know what came over him," Allegra murmured.

The last vestige of what Sister Therese called an epiphany fled. *So this was his way of letting a girl know that his bellowed "Get out. Get out and stay out" meant just that. So this was the time for that wishy-washy girl to start forgetting that she had ever known a boy named Bruce Seerie. Good-bye, buster. It was nice knowing the Bruce I thought you were. But it's not so nice knowing whatever Bruce you are now.*

Claude McIntosh came hurrying in just as the crowd was dispersing. Stacy made a point of introducing him to Allegra and Jake, and of drawing Allegra aside to say, "He's a grand fellow. He sent one of the bunches of flowers. Goodness, I forgot to ask. Have you heard from Robbie?"

"Not yet. But I will. Maybe I'll get a whole batch of letters all at once. That's the way overseas mail is."

Stacy rode home with Claude. He *was* a grand fellow to squeeze the price of carnations out of his tight budget. As a start on her forget-Bruce program, she kissed him good-night—a real kiss instead of the usual smack on the cheek she allotted him. It was a test kiss, and in it was her hope that she might be stirred to feel greater fondness for him.

It left her unstirred, but he hugged her tighter. "How about an encore?" he insisted.

She ducked expertly. "I'm dog-tired, Claude, and Mom's waiting to postmortem the whole show."

On Sunday, in rented caps and gowns and with each graduate escorted to the altar by a junior, the senior class of St. Jude's received their diplomas.

That night Claire gave her long-promised and long-delayed party—an outdoor supper—to celebrate the removal of the barbed wire from her teeth. After appetites had been satisfied, they sat around the smoking barbecue grill, and reminisced and laughed heartily but a little sadly about all the various happenings that had occurred during the four years they had traipsed together through the halls of St. Jude's.

Stacy reminded them of the time Obie had been clowning at the blackboard and the nun teaching them had reproved him by giving him a tap on the head with the book she held, and of how Obie had rolled up his eyes and dropped to the floor. For one aghast moment, the nun had thought her tap on the head had brought on a concussion. It was the titter from the class that had reassured her.

"And then she gave me a real whack," Obie remembered.

And of course somebody had to bring up one of Stacy's most hilarious word garblings. It had happened last year when there had been a young seminarian at St. Jude's who coached basketball and taught religion. He had also delighted in what he called "Stacyisms," and had told her that he often regaled his fellow theological students with them. It was during his oral drill on the sacrament of baptism that in answer to his question, "What is chrism?" Stacy had promptly recited, "Chrism is a holy oil secreted by the bishop." Not only had the class laughed, but the teacher had so doubled up with mirth he could hardly correct her. "The bishop *consecrates* the oil, Stacy—" He had to stop and give a few more guffaws before he could wipe his eyes and find breath to add, "It would keep him pretty busy *secreting* enough for all the baptisms."

One guest at Claire's backyard party was a little outside the circle. It was partly because he had only entered St. Jude's this past year and partly because of his exaggerated sideburns which were trimmed in something the shape of a question mark.

He was the closest thing to a boy friend Claire had ever had, even though she was realist enough to know that he always turned on his charm and attention when he needed her help on a book review. "Maybe he'll ask me for dates when I get my barbed wire off," she had said hopefully to Stacy.

He, unable to share the reminiscences of the past, turned the talk to the near future. He was to deliver a car to San Francisco for one of the drive-a-car companies.

There was talk then of trips, of scholarships, of summer jobs. Liesel spilled over about how she would move out of the dingy quarters behind the delicatessen shop and her father's strict jurisdiction in just four more days, when she was eighteen, and how she would make her home with Jean Patrice, the dress designer and importer. "I'll take care of her little girl and the house while Jean Patrice goes on a buying trip to Europe."

Claire mentioned her summer library job and the further good news that her brother was selling her his old car and letting her pay for it out of her salary.

Stacy added her voice to the others. "I've got a job too, I think, singing in a supper club. A girl that works there made enough in two months to buy a car."

Claire said again what she had said when Stacy had mentioned it to her before, "I'll just bet Ben and your mother will raise ructions about your singing in a nightclub. Does Ben think it's okay?"

"He doesn't know about it. I'll wait till he goes on his road-construction job tomorrow, and then—then I'm just sure I can soften up Mom. After all, she entertains at Guido's."

"Where is this place and what's the name of it?" someone else asked her.

"I can't remember the name—or where it is. I've been so busy being Bernadette. But it's all on the card I've got tucked away. I remember it's thirty miles and thirty minutes from Denver. And the owner's first name is Mike. I remember that." She looked around at the familiar friendly faces and added, "Isn't it great for us all to have such rosy plans? Just like the title of that Dickens book we had to read last year—*Great Expectorations.*"

There was the usual stunned and bewildered lull that always followed one of what the young seminarian called a Stacyism. And then came the ha-ha-ha's and the shrieks of laughter. Someone sputtered out that expecting was slightly different from spitting.

And Obie, swabbing the tears on his cheek with his knuckles, said weakly, "Ah, what will the world be to us when Stacy and belly laughs are no more?"

17 ❧

C*LAIRE* called for Stacy the next morning in her newly acquired but far from new car. "Imagine me—minus braces and plus a car and a job," she gloated. "My cup runneth over."

The one minus and two plusses did indeed seem to transform the ugly duckling of St. Jude's into a confident, even cocky, young woman of the world.

They set out in the car to return their rented caps and gowns to the costume company downtown. "I want my deposit back right away as long as I'm leaving town tomorrow," Claire said.

"Ben wants back the deposit he paid on mine, right away too."

"And then I'll take my car up to Mac's garage for a grease job," Claire continued.

My car. Stacy had the first twinge of envy she had ever felt for her staunch friend. "It won't take me long to get a car once I start on my job," she said. "Mike said that what Guido paid us for entertaining was peanuts." Her cup too would runneth over when she got her hands on the wheel of her own car.

They rode home with their refunds through the first hot day in June. Even though Claire demurred that she had a million things to do, Stacy persuaded her to stop at the Belfords' for iced tea. "I want to show you the card Mike gave me."

They carried their clinking glasses of tea up to the small room at the head of the stairs. Stacy pulled out the shallow top drawer of the dresser and said as she rattled through its contents, "I didn't even have a chance to read it because of old nosy-posy Jill." More frantic scrabbling and clacking of bottles and lipsticks. "Gosh, I remember sliding it under this velvet box. And I remember seeing a corner of it when— Where in the world could it—?"

"Pull out the whole drawer. Maybe it worked under the paper lining. It couldn't have walked away."

Stacy yanked out the drawer. She dumped its debris onto the bed. She lifted the mussed paper on the bottom and shook it.

No card.

With Claire's help she pulled the dresser away from the wall so as to look behind and beneath it. Still no sign of a small stiff white rectangle.

Stacy stood in hard-breathing dismay. She could hear Jill in the side yard under the open window. Jill had times of reverting to her tomboy self, and this morning she was arguing heatedly with Matt about something to do with her bicycle. Stacy called down to her, "Jill, Jill! Did you do anything with a little white card I had in my top drawer?"

"A what?"

"You heard me." But she repeated with loud stern emphasis, "A little white card. It was in my top drawer under that velvet box."

"What would I want with an old card?"

"I'm not asking what you'd want with it. I'm asking if you saw it or took it."

Jill shouted back, "Well, ask in one hand and spit in the other and see which gets full the soonest," and turned back to her ferocious argument with Matt.

"That stinker. If I thought—"

"Why would she take it?" Claire mollified her. "Sometimes a little thing like a card can work through a crack in the back of a drawer. Maybe it's fallen into the next drawer. Didn't this Mike tell you the name of the place?"

Stacy pawed frantically through the drawer under the top one—this time through a melee of underthings. "There was so much racket out there at Guido's and he was talking so fast." She gave a frowning moment of concentration. "Seems to me it was the name of a bird —a sort of pretty name. Maybe if we looked in the yellow pages—"

"It'd be like hunting for the needle in the haystack. And if it's thirty miles and thirty minutes from Denver, it wouldn't be in our directory." Claire stood up. "I've got to get my car to Mac's. Look, hon, maybe it's all for the best that you can't find it. Somehow it never sounded quite kosher to me." She added from the doorway, "You won't have any trouble getting a job."

It was Jill's very avoidance of her the rest of the day that aroused Stacy's suspicions. In the late afternoon she managed to corner her in the garage, and found out the awful truth.

Yes, Jill had seen the little old card—but how did she know Stacy thought it was the only card in the whole world? And Jill had needed *something* to try out Stacy's lipsticks on, to find one that looked real light so Sister would believe her when she said it was salve—

"Where's the card now?"

"Well, it was all streaked with lipstick. And that was a long, long time ago, and how did I know—"

"What did you do with the card, you dirty little sneak?"

After much squirming and twisting and well-ing, Jill admitted she had dropped it into the wastebasket.

A faint hope pushed through Stacy's fury. "Did you read what was on it?"

A chastened Jill shook her head. She had evidently been too intent and too hurried in her testing of lipsticks.

Stacy's groan came from her soul. It was indeed a long time ago that Jill had felt compelled to outdo her competitor for Itsy Sullivan's attention, a long time ago since the wicker wastebasket in their room would have been emptied with the card. Stacy gritted out, "I could hang you by your thumbs—yes, and dance around you while you were hanging. You've ruined my whole life."

In her desperation she sought out her mother who was upstairs replacing the winter blanket on her bed with a summer one.

"Mom, that St. Patrick's Day night out at Guido's there was a man there and he told me he ran a night-

club too. I just thought maybe you might know him—
or have met him. He had black slicked-down hair, and
he had on a vest—sort of a fancy one. I thought maybe
Guido might have mentioned him or introduced him.
His name was Mike."

Mother shook her head blankly. "No. I don't remember meeting anyone like that. Why?"

"He gave me a card, and that monster in my room"
—Stacy ground her teeth—"threw it away. He liked my
singing. And I just thought I might phone him about a
job. He said for me to."

"In a nightclub! Oh, no, Stacy. Ben would hit the
ceiling if—"

"So he'd hit the ceiling," she hurled out. "And I hope
he'd wham his head hard on it. *You* entertain in a
nightclub."

Mother tucked in a corner of the blanket before she
straightened up. "Guido's is different. He only serves
wine and beer. Oh, lovey, Guido's is like a Sunday
school picnic compared to most nightclubs. Believe me,
some of those with their topless waitresses—they really
are what preachers call dens of iniquity. "You won't
have any trouble finding a summer job," she went on
soothingly. "Go through the want ads. Remember last
summer how lucky you were?"

Yes, last summer she had been lucky. She had answered an ad, "Unusual job for unusual girl," and
found herself with the unusual job of chauffeuring for
an irascible but lovable old cattleman.

The next morning Stacy thumbed through the two
pages of *Help Wanted* ads in the morning *Call*. What

in the world was a Friden Flexowriter or a PBX or Key Punch Operator? RN meant registered nurse, which Stacy was not, but what was an LPN? She was neither a dental hygienist nor a beautician with following. Nurse's aides were wanted but "must furn own transp," meaning they needed to have their own car. So did concession workers in the amusement parks which were located far out on the edge of town.

"That lets me out," she said resentfully to Ben across the table. He was using the family Chevvy to get to his summer road-building job and back.

"Keep on looking," he said.

All too many of the requirements let her out. Her age, for one. Nineteen to twenty-five appeared with regularity in the ads. She skipped over the long list of cocktail waitresses and barmaids. Even if she were old enough, Ben would hit the proverbial ceiling on those.

"Typists 50 wpm." A few employers would even settle for "45 wpm." Maybe with some concentrated practice she could qualify. The Novaks across the street had a much newer typewriter than Ben's. "Sure, Stacy, just come over and help yourself to it," Mrs. Novak told her.

For one whole day she copied letters and pages from books. The best speed she could work up to was twenty-two words per minute. And in the twenty-two she made three mistakes.

While she was there, Mrs. Novak told her of the trip to Iowa she and her husband were planning to take the week after next. Her younger sister was to be married. Could Stacy move over and take care of the children for the six days they would be gone? "There'll only be three," for they were taking the five-year-old with them to be a flower girl at the wedding. They would fly, and Stacy would have the use of their car in their absence.

"You know the house so well, and you manage these ornery brats better than anyone else I know," Mrs. Novak ended.

"Stacy, you come. You stay with us," the brats clamored.

Yes, Stacy agreed. She would take care of them if she didn't get a job before that. Although she grumbled about being sick, sick, sick of baby-sitting, actually she enjoyed it. She felt at home with children, and they with her. But what kind of a career was off-and-on baby-sitting jobs?

All that week and into the next, Stacy sat at the phone or answered ads in person. "Models Wanted." For that interview she washed her hair, put on eye makeup and her most glamorous clothes, only to find that until she had taken a sixty-day training course to the tune of $197.50 the job was not available. Another ad read "No exp nec. Only persistence, personality, and a smile." But the interview there revealed that it was selling burglar-alarm systems from door to door.

And then opportunity knocked, and what is more, it knocked even with "oppt for adv," as the ads put it, meaning opportunity for advancement. The knock came through Claude McIntosh. The downtown department store where he sold shoes was having a two-day sale of cobra-skin pumps—Not real cobra, he admitted. Matching bags and belts would also be featured at a counter adjoining the shoe department, and Claude had persuaded his manager to hire Stacy to sell them. He told Stacy enthusiastically that if she did a bang-up job selling bags and belts—"Don't ever think the management doesn't check up on new salesgirls"—why then she'd be given another spot in the store. In time she could even work up to buyer. There was a big future in merchandising.

The first day Stacy made mistakes. She put charge-a-plates in the metal machine backward. She figured the sales tax wrong. There was a great to-do because she let one customer walk out with a cobra-skin bag before the office could send back word that the woman's charge account had been discontinued.

Claude, all business in the shoe department, even scolded her about it. "But she was in a hurry," Stacy explained. "And she wanted to carry the bag to a luncheon."

"Don't let them rush you. You can always phone the office and give the name and address, and they'll tell you whether or not the customer can take the purchase. You'll do better tomorrow," he added.

She didn't. She was no pusher of wares. She couldn't help identifying herself sympathetically with her customers. To her the price of the bags—between thirty-two and thirty-six dollars—was exorbitant. A sixteen-year-old girl with her tired and plainly dressed mother stopped at the counter. She turned over and opened first one large rectangular purse and then a squat puffy one, saying greedily, "I'd just love one for my birthday." Stacy saw the counting-up look in the mother's eyes and said, "Yes, but I'll bet none of your friends would know the difference between these and the two-ninety-five ones in the basement."

Claude heard her. He saw mother and daughter turn to take the down escalator to the basement.

"Don't ever mention a cheaper article," he coached her. "Stress the fittings, the lasting quality of the superior article. And besides"—his boyish grin took away the sting—"don't ever say *basement*. Say *economy floor*."

Stacy spent too much time visiting with "lookers" who had no intention of buying. She even listened to a long-winded old gentleman telling of his homestead days on the plains and of his killing not cobras but rattlesnakes and making belts and hat bands out of their hides.

She knew when her two-day stint was over, even without Claude telling her, that her sales ability would *not* call her to the attention of the higher-ups.

Oddly enough her failure seemed to inflate rather than deflate Claude. "Don't you worry one little bit. I've got enough push and know-how for both of us."

At times like this, Stacy realized that her test kiss hadn't been so wise after all. It had proved to her that there would never be any breathtaking heights—or black depths—for her with him, but he seemed to take it for granted that they would one day share life on an unlimited budget with waiters bobbing about to ask if everything was "all right, sir."

"I don't like selling things," she lamented wearily and defiantly at supper that evening.

"Neither do I," her mother confessed. "I'd much rather give things away."

"Just what *would* you like to do, Miss Pick-and-Choose?" Ben demanded.

Stacy gave him a baleful glance. "I don't know."

She suddenly hated the ones that did know: Claude and his merchandizing, Ben and his doctoring, his after-school and weekend work at the Ragged Robin and his harder road-building job in summer, which he did without a grumble because of his goal.

Jeanie Kincaid, too with her eyes on a newspaper career was bustling about getting news and social items for a suburban weekly. And Katie Rose was with a summer opera group that would be touring some of the smaller cities. She wrote home, "I'm an understudy for the second lead, and doing scenery and properties— just anything. But I'm learning theater from the ground up."

But she, Stacy Belford, was the grasshopper who had frittered away not the summer but her four years at St. Jude's with never a thought for the future. She hadn't learned about the card system in the library or stayed after school to perfect her typing as Claire had. Oh, no, she had gone streaking down those worn old school steps toward a waiting car, toward a dark-haired boy who always climbed out from behind the wheel at sight of her and came hurrying to meet her.

So now she was a washout. The boy she had fought with and made up with and fed ducks with and laughed with and danced with was giving her the go-by. And so was life.

(185)

18 ❧

ON SUNDAY Stacy took over her six-day stint of looking after the Novak domain and the three small Novak boys. That afternoon she drove the whole family to the airport. And how Sissy, the flower-girl-to-be, lorded it over her stay-at-home brothers, especially over Chip, her elder by two years. *She* was going to fly. *She* was going to a wedding. *She* was going to eat supper on a plane.

The Novak parents in a final fluster of do's and don'ts said good-bye. Mr. Novak in high spirits called back to Stacy, "Don't drink up all my booze while I'm gone."

Chip, his ego quite deflated, sulked all the way home. As they went into the house, he asked, "Did you ever go to a wedding, Stacy?"

"Yes, three or four times."

"What's a wedding like?"

"Just like church," Stacy told him. "Except for the bride and her father marching up the aisle and the groom standing there, waiting for them. And then church goes on and on, and kids have to sit still just the way they do on Sundays. And everybody keeps wishing it would hurry up and be over so they could leave."

"Will Sissy have to stay still all that time?"

"Oh, yes. Stiller than anybody."

"Did you ever have supper on a plane?

"No, but I know what it's like. Like eating anyplace else except you eat off a tray. Except if you want another roll or piece of cake, you don't get it. Tell you what, we'll eat our supper on trays, and it'll be just like Sissy and your mom and dad."

She served them scrambled eggs and cocoa on trays, and Chip took special satisfaction in asking for two more cupcakes. "I just wish Sissy would ask for another piece of cake, and the boss on the plane would tell her to go blow."

What a joy it was to have a car to back out of the garage and go places in. Stacy took her charges the next day to a wading pool in the small Mamie Eisenhower park and to see a Charlie Brown movie. They all went calling on Mrs. Novak's mother the following afternoon, and she gave the children money to stop at a dairy bar for ice cream.

Stacy even took them with her to the Belford mansion when she went to visit Grandfather Belford. He had returned from Phoenix, and Mother had already called. "Oh, Stacy, he looks so frail. He's in bed most of the day. And so lonely in that big old mausoleum with only Emil and the housekeeper. Stop in if you get a minute. Wouldn't you think that flibbertigibbet Eustace would come home and look after him instead of staying on for the point-to-point races—whatever those fool things are—in Godalming." And she spat out again, "Godalming! Godalmighty!"

The young Novaks were fascinated by the iron wolf trying to down the iron deer, and by the goldfish darting among the water lilies in the pool. Emil, Grandfather's general factotum, was trimming the hedges, and he said, "I'll keep an eye on them out here, Miss Stacy, while you visit the old gentleman." He opened the door for her and told her she'd find him in his upstairs room. "He's sitting up for awhile."

Stacy walked softly through the long tiled reception hall and up the winding stairs. Grandfather's door was ajar, and she took a hesitant step inside, thinking he might be asleep.

He was sitting in an upholstered chair, a heavy book resting on his knees. It was the first time Stacy had ever seen him when he wasn't dressed, as befitted a scholarly gentleman and retired chancellor of the university, in a dark suit with a white or pale-colored shirt and conservative tie. His suits always seemed to have vests, and his shoes always to be newly polished.

It was something of a shock to see him in a robe and soft slippers. His hair, like fine silk floss, bore the marks of a comb. His skin was like tissue paper that had been crumpled up and then smoothed out.

His eyes lighted when he saw her. "Stacy, my dear, come in. Come in and sit down."

She took his long thin fingers—why, they were cold!

—and in a sudden rush of emotion dropped down on the footstool that went with the chair, still warming his hand in hers. "Am I interrupting your reading?"

"No, no. I'm just renewing my acquaintance with my old friend Occleve or Hoccleve, an early fifteenth-century poet who never got the recognition he was entitled to. Imagine his writing a fifty-five-hundred-line treatise in rhyme royal to Prince Hal."

Stacy couldn't imagine it.

"But I'd far rather look at you and hear your laugh," he said gallantly. "So tell me all about Stacy."

"There's nothing to tell. I don't amount to much."

"Don't say that."

"I can't even get a job. I'm just plain stupid." It was a relief to pour out to a wise and neutral ear all the jobs she had been unable to get and her miserable failure as a saleswoman of cobra bags and belts.

"What are you happy doing? Maybe happiness is the wrong word. What gives you an inner content and satisfaction?" Grandfather Belford asked.

Inner content and satisfaction. That was how she had felt that evening with Jake when she told the story of the rebuffed little skunk to the hard-breathing children in the asthmatic ward. "I like being with kids— with children," she said, and added with a rueful laugh, "Maybe that's because I'm mentally retarded."

He chuckled softly. "No, not that. Let me tell you, my dear. Whenever I used to talk to the graduates about what in those days we called 'making something of yourself,' I tried to tell them that the real reward came from giving something of yourself. The world is full of givers and of takers. And your family, Stacy, are all givers."

The housekeeper interrupted by pushing in a tea cart with Grandfather's afternoon tea. She would get an extra cup for Stacy.

No, Stacy said, she couldn't stay that long; she must hurry along with the children. "I'm surprised they're still on their good behavior out there with Emil. But I'll come for tea when I don't have them to worry about," she added.

The housekeeper maneuvered the tea cart close to Grandfather's knees, filled his cup, and after exchanging a few amenities with them both, departed.

Stacy glanced at the tea things. Yes, there were the lemon slices stuck with cloves, the bite-size sandwiches, and *petits fours*. She thought of Mother's first tea at the Belford mansion when her sister-in-law-to-be had spoken loftily of Iturbi and Tchaikovsky. The words slipped out. "Mother thinks Aunt Eustace looks down her nose at her."

"Oh, dear, that was a tactless thing to say. But Grandfather's eyes twinkled roguishly. "Eustace is jealous of her."

"Jealous of Mother! Oh, no."

"So jealous she can taste it," he said with relish.

"But why on earth—"

"Because your mother is warm and loving and real, because she goes at life without gloves on. While Eustace— It's a terrible thing, my child, not to become a woman when one ceases to be a girl. Eustace at fifty

—or thereabouts—still holds on to being the reigning queen. I forgot who said, 'The thoughts of youth are long, long thoughts.' Yes, yes, but the thoughts of an idle old person are longer. Eustace is the one your mother should feel pity for, just as I do in my long, long thoughts."

Small running footsteps pounded up the tiled stairs, and Chip's voice called out, "Hey, Stacy—wherever you are. Budge wet his pants, and he keeps pulling them off. Emil said you better take him home."

Hastily she kissed her grandfather's papery cheek and departed.

On Thursday as a special treat, Stacy fixed a picnic lunch and drove the three boys to City Park. They visited the children's zoo, the playgrounds, the ride on the miniature train. Budge's short legs soon gave out, and Stacy carried him. The grand finale in the late afternoon was the boat ride around the lake on a launch called the *City of Denver*, which was as impressive to all the small passengers as the *Queen Mary* would have been.

Stacy had just settled herself with the heavy weight of Budge on her lap on one of the seats in the long wooden benches that ran along both sides of the boat when a sudden small cyclone descended upon her, a small cyclone in a scanty sunsuit who caught Stacy around the knees with gurgles of delight. It was Mary Liz Buell.

"It's Stacy—it's Stacy. Look, Mister. Look, Miz Tilden. It's Stacy."

Close behind her was Mister who explained in his sober way, "We stayed at a nursery school today, and we're going to tomorrow too. Because there's a convention, and Mother likes to go to things with her husband."

A young woman, a little on the plump side, her blond hair in disarray and her arms full of caps and sweaters, had seated herself on the long bench across from Stacy. She seemed quite unperturbed by all her charges—five, to six, besides the two Buells—scrambling for seats on first one side of the boat and then the other.

Stacy smiled at her. "I often baby-sit for Mary Liz and Mister."

"She sings for us. She dances for us," Mary Liz repeated three times.

"And plays music too sometimes," Mister contributed.

The motor boat skimmed over the lake, criss-crossing the fountain in the middle. Over the shrieks of childish delight each time a carp bobbed out of the water, Stacy and the young woman talked.

The name of the young woman was Donna Tilden, and she ran a day camp, Stacy discovered. This carload which she had brought with her to the park were the ones that needed to be picked up at their homes in the morning and delivered there again in the evening at six. The rest of her twenty-seven pupils were brought and called for by their parents. "That little girl," she said, indicating a slim first grader in orange shorts, "is my own Tammie."

The baby in Stacy's lap dozed. The slightly older Timmy fell in one of his rushes across the boat and skinned his knee. Stacy comforted him, "I'll put medicine on it when we get home."

The director of the day camp dug into the capacious bag on her lap and produced a bottle of Mercurochrome. She pulled Timmy onto her lap to apply it. "I carry such things for emergencies," she said serenely.

At the boat's docking there was the inevitable clamor for another ride. But Stacy and Mrs. Tilden herded them off and toward their cars. The station wagon with JOHNNY APPLESEED DAY CAMP printed on its door was parked close to the Novak car. Stacy shifted her burden of drowsy child to the flattish hood of the station wagon while she and the young woman continued to talk.

Yes, Mrs. Tilden said, she knew Carleton and Beany Buell. She didn't have their children regularly but was keeping them today and tomorrow so that Beany could go to some of the luncheons and meetings at the law convention with her husband. "The nursery is closed on Saturday and Sunday.

"Pile in, the whole caboodle of you," she told the fringe of children. "We're already a little late." She climbed in herself and leaned over to put her key into the ignition. Stacy took the now squirming toddler into her arms. She stepped back, holding Timmy's hand. A glance told her that Chip was already waiting beside the Novak car.

Mrs. Tilden stepped on the starter. It gave only a rackety whir. Her eyes and Stacy's looked at the gas gauge. It was at the three-quarter mark. She tried again and again. Each time there was only a clackety-clack—and then nothing.

"Does it sound like the battery's dead to you, Stacy?"

"Or else something's disconnected."

Whatever it was, the car wouldn't start. Donna Tilden pushed open the door and looked toward the out-door telephone near the boathouse. "If you want to phone for help, go ahead," Stacy said. "I'll watch the children."

"I'll call Mac's garage. Maybe he can tell me what to do. Or maybe send his helper over right away."

Her face was less serene when she returned. "Mac says it sounds like the starter. He'll have to wait till his helper gets back to send him. I don't know what to do about delivering these children."

Stacy looked toward the Novaks' Ford and gauged the space the eight squirmers in the station wagon and her own three would take. "I think I can pack them all in. This little fellow will sit in his car seat."

"Oh, could you, Stacy? Just seven, because you wouldn't mind waiting with me, would you, Tam?"

The amiable Tam wouldn't mind.

"It won't be so crowded when you let Mister and Mary Liz Buell out, and then these two boys"— indicating two in battered straw hats—"live just a block behind Laurel Lane. I'll jot down the addresses. And, Stacy, wait until someone opens the door for each child."

She jotted down addresses on the back of a card on which was printed:

JOHNNY APPLESEED

DAY CAMP

Ages three to eight

Hours seven to six

HOT LUNCH ● NAPTIME ● PLAYTIME

FENCED PLAYGROUND ● CONSTANT

SUPERVISION

Donna S. Tilden, *Director*

The passengers tumbled out of the station wagon and raced toward the cream-colored car. Budge was wedged protestingly into his car seat. The two other Novaks refused to give up their front seat with Stacy. "Mary Liz can ride up here," Chip said. It wasn't *too* crowded with six small ones in the backseat.

Stacy delivered the two Buells first. Their mother, still in her dress-up clothes, opened the door for them, and Stacy waved and called out, "I'm pinch-hitting for Mrs. Tilden."

The straw-hatted ones were let out next. Stacy studied the addresses and, one by one, deposited the other three at their doors.

She swung back to the park to see if the Johnny Appleseed car had been put in working order. It hadn't. The service truck from Mac's Garage was pulled up in front of it, and Mac's helper was rattling out a tow chain.

"He's sure it's the starter," Donna Tilden said. "He'll tow it in, and Mac will phone to let me know if he can have it ready in the morning."

"So you'll have to take us home too," Tammie said.

"Sure, I will. Get in."

Donna crowded into the front seat and shifted Timmie of the skinned knee onto her lap. "Stacy, you've been a lifesaver. I had visions of paying out a big chunk for taxiing all those youngsters home. But I'll pay you just the same."

"Oh, no. I love to drive. Just pay for the gas, because I *have* used up some of the tankful Mr. Novak left."

Following Donna's directions, Stacy found her way and stopped in the side driveway of a roomy house that would be taken for a family residence except for the wooden sign in the front yard: "Johnny Appleseed Day Camp."

"It's what you call a two-level house," Donna murmured.

Tammie bragged to the Novak boys, "We've got a new merry-go-round, and it isn't as big, but it's prettier than the ones at the park."

"We want to see it," they chorused.

"You'll have time to stop a minute, won't you, Stacy, for a Coke or whatever?"

"I'd like to see your day camp."

The top floor, Stacy saw, was living quarters for Donna and Tammie. Wide steps led down to rooms that were half below ground, half above. All was quiet and neat with the last child, the last instructor, gone.

They passed through the rectangular room used for dancing classes and recreation, and the schoolroom with small chairs and tables, its walls covered by childish crayon drawings. "We only put up the gay ones," Donna said. "Sometimes they turn out pretty morbid ones."

Stacy stood in the doorway of the "sleeproom" with its multitude of beds like army cots, only child-size. These walls were not the off-white of the other rooms but a soft green, and the curtains, instead of filmy white, were a darker green that could be drawn together.

Tammie was at the mammoth refrigerator in the kitchen pulling out a freezer tray of frozen Popsicles for herself and guests. "I make them out of fruit juice," Donna murmured.

This room was both kitchen and dining room. A long table that would seat thirty children occupied one end of it. "I always fix the lunch," Donna said, "and, believe me, I've learned what small children prefer in the way of food."

While Tammie and the Novak boys occupied themselves in the playground behind the house, Donna and Stacy sat on the screened porch and drank Cokes.

The telephone interrupted. The call was from Mac to report that he couldn't possibly have her starter fixed before Saturday. He had too many other jobs to do ahead of it. But she could count on it by Monday for sure. Stacy overhearing Donna's "But, Mac, I need transportation for eight children *tomorrow*" hastened to interrupt. "I can pick them up for you in the morning and take them back in the evening."

"That's asking *too* much, Stacy."

"Oh, no. Honest, I'd be glad to. Maybe I could drop the boys off here in the morning so the car wouldn't be so crowded."

"Of course, you could." Donna sat down and picked up her Coke. "But Gwen, the girl who handles recreation for us, asked for two weeks off to go to California with friends. I thought the other staffworkers and I could double for her while she was gone. But it's too much for us. It's not fair to the children either."

"But you'll have two children less next week. I mean Mary Liz and Mister."

Donna laughed. "No, we'll have three more. Another family I know asked if I could take the children while they painted and varnished their whole downstairs." She fiddled thoughtfully a moment with her Coke bottle. "Stacy, are you busy next week? Could you help us out till Gwen gets back?

Stacy gasped on her swallow of Coke. "I'm not busy —but do you think I'd be good enough? Don't you have to have special training in things like child psychology—and games—and—"

"Not to be a helper. We'll show you the ropes. And you have such a wonderful way with children. You *relate*, as they say nowadays."

She briefed her a little more. Stacy would have to have a chest X ray. The Board of Health was very strict about that for anyone who worked with children. With her unruffled efficiency, she phoned the nearby Colorado General Hospital.

"Anytime tomorrow between ten and three," she reported to Stacy. "And they'll bill the day camp." She added with her easy laugh, "You'll do all right. I'll tell you what I always keep in mind—it's what a Montessori lecturer said when I was taking nursery-school training. Always remember, he said, that it isn't enough to keep young bodies active and busy. Minds and hearts have to grow and expand too. When you have storytime with them, it isn't enough to tell them stories. Let them tell you stories too. Their time at the playground is more than playtime. It's learning to be fair and kind and helpful. Oh, yes, and I'll tell Mac to deliver the station wagon to you on Hubbell for you to have Monday morning. You keep it there, so's to save your having to come here for it."

"Oh, I know I'll like it," Stacy breathed.

19 ∾

S _T A C Y_ did indeed like everything about her fill-in job at the day camp. There was an incentive now to leap out of bed in the morning before the alarm finished its ring. She liked the experience of guiding the station wagon through the early morning streets, of seeing young Appleseeders waiting outside for a sight of it or, at the gentle tap of her horn, bolting out the door and racing toward it. She liked letting them off in the evening when perhaps a father would halt from his lawn mowing or a mother open a screen door in welcome.

Stacy's mother, on vacation from Guido's, went to Bannon to visit old friends and see and hear Katie Rose in summer opera. When Grandda O'Byrne drove in from Bannon for her on Monday, he brought Liz with him to stay with the Belford family while she was gone.

Liz was a comfortable person to have around with her belief that growing children needed stews and apple tarts, with her good-night "May God sleep on your pillow," and her shopping for yarn and knitting a Rose of Sharon afghan for some kinswoman soon to be married.

And so was the director of the day camp a comfortable person to work for. Donna Tilden kept to no strict routine. The instructors' jobs often overlapped.

Stacy made friends with the slim graceful black girl who taught dancing and who doubled with Stacy in taking the twenty older children on tours of a firehouse and museum. A university athlete came four days a week to handle games and take them swimming. He came after a day off with such a painful sunburn from playing tennis that Stacy swapped chores with him. She took a load of children in his souped-up car to the outdoor swimming pool while he, his back and shoulders covered with ointment, stood in the shade and supervised playground activities.

Another noontime when Donna's class in the schoolroom was still in the thick of gluing seashells on matchboxes, she asked Stacy to start the luncheon meal of macaroni and cheese.

On Thursday when it was time for Stacy to deliver her eight, squirming, chattering passengers, thunder roared and rumbled overhead louder than a jet plane. The rain came pounding down even before she had made her first stop with the three whose house was in the paint-and-varnish process.

She found a rumpled raincoat in a corner of the backseat and shook it out as best she could. It made scanty covering for the three. Stacy raced to the door with them in order to retrieve it.

At her next three stops a member of the family was watching for the car and came out with an umbrella to protect the returnee. No one however, was waiting for a little girl in a sunsuit consisting mostly of a few ruffles. She was too afraid of the still crackling thunder to leave the car. Stacy bundled the raincoat around her and carried her to her door.

The last passenger to be left off was always six-year-old Walter. Walter, who wore a visored baseball cap pulled down over belligerent eyes, was the only one on the playground who kicked his playmates in the shins. He was the only one who never answered Stacy's good morning when he climbed into the car in the morning or her good-bye when he climbed out in the evening.

Donna's small Tammie, who seemed to be all eyes and ears, had told her, "He never did to Gwen either. He didn't like her a bit. Once he spilled cocoa in her lap exactly on purpose." She added, "He's got a brother and sister that are a whole lot older than him. His mother says he was a little postscript they didn't expect. She sells houses to people."

"That's enough, Tammie," her mother said.

This wet evening Walter refused Stacy's offer of the raincoat and stalked his own splashy way along the flagstone path. She watched him try the door and find it locked as usual. No doubt, his mother was somewhere unlocking other doors to show houses to prospective buyers. Stacy watched him stalk on to a neighbor's house two doors down where a door admitted him.

Stacy was soaked, her feet slippery in wet sandals on

the car pedals. The downpour slackened to what was only a drizzle by the time she reached Hubbell Street.

Matt, Brian, *and* Cully had evidently raced home through the rain from a baseball game for Stacy was met by the sight and smell of wet baseball shoes, mitts, *and* dog. She was starting up the stairs to take off her own wet T-shirt and shorts when Jill came in from the kitchen.

"Liz told me to watch the stew while she went downtown to buy yarn and stuff. She told me not to let it cook dry, and I kept putting in water. You come out, Stacy, and see—"

Stacy squashed her way into the kitchen. The kettle of stew was full to the brim with grayish-brown water.

"She told me to be careful and not let it burn."

"She didn't mean for you to drown it in water, you stupe. Leave the lid off, and maybe it'll cook down." Stacy started again for the stairs.

The front door opened letting in a gust of rain-drenched air and a glimpse of a red and white taxi in front of the house. Liz came in laden with bundles and puffing for breath. "My, my, but I was lucky to find a nice taxi driver. I don't know how I'd have managed—"

With that, the nice taxi driver, obliterated except for his cap by the burden in his arms, entered. He was carrying a six-foot-high tree with shiny green leaves and here and there a sprinkling of yellow lemons. It was housed in a rectangular tub of cedar or redwood held together by wide brass hoops.

Jill screeched out, "Is that a lemon tree?" and Matt, halfway down the stairs, sneered, "What do you *think* lemons grow on?" Liz was saying, "Here, son, just put it down close to the piano so we won't be bumping it. Get away, Cully. I always wanted a lemon tree to put in my bay window. Stacy, love, move your guitar."

She picked up the guitar which gave a gentle twang. The driver set down the tree, straightened up, and brushed a little black loam from his hands. Stacy felt her heart do that old familiar double-flip under her ribs as he took a backward step toward the door and pulled off the cap from his dark mat of hair.

She stared at him, and he stared back out of veiled expressionless eyes. She managed to squeak out, "Hi, Bruce," and he answered, "How's it going, Stacy?" in a neutral voice that showed no interest in learning how it was going with Stacy.

This Bruce Seerie was a still different one from the Bruce she had called a donkey who followed a carrot, a different one from the Bruce who had drunkenly gripped her wrist at the Student Union party and threatened Claude, and a far cry from the Bruce in the messy basement who had sneered at her offering of sympathy and bellowed at her to get out and stay out.

This Bruce looked thinner and older. His unsmiling face had a fined-down look that showed the bones beneath it. His broad shoulders were just as broad but not so padded with flesh, and yet—and yet he didn't seem too different from the Bruce Stacy had first known, or maybe imagined, the Bruce she had looked up to and been drawn to.

What could Stacy say to him or he to her with Liz fumbling through the disorder in her purse for her taxi fare and tip, with the audience of three looking with wonder not only at the lemon tree but at Bruce in his taxi driver's garb of gray denim shirt and slacks.

Liz pressed the money into his palm, and on her affable "I'll call you again when I need you," he smiled his thanks, put his cap back on his head and left.

Stacy sank weakly down on the piano bench still holding the guitar. He could have said good-bye to her, couldn't he? He could have said something besides that meaningless, "How's it going?" couldn't he?

He and Liz had evidently talked together a great deal on the long drive from downtown. She told Stacy about it all the while she was tch-tching over the thin brew on the stove and draining a quart of water off it. "When I told him where I lived, he said he used to know you, Stacy. And then I recognized him and I said, 'You're Bruce. Imagine my not knowing you!'"

He used to know her.

"The poor boy works so hard. He says he tries to get on the night shift because the tips are better then. And when he gets a day off, he goes up and works on a cabin in the mountains."

Jake's, I suppose.

"I told him I didn't think he ate enough," Liz went on. "But then a fellow isn't apt to when he doesn't have anyone to cook for him. I told him if he ever had time to stop in here, and I'd fix him a good filling meal."

Fat chance of Bruce doing that!

"And I told him all about the family. I knew he'd want to hear."

Oh, you did, did you? Maybe you told him that poor

Stacy wasn't smart enough to get a job except to fill in here and there. And that she had a beau named Claude who budgets his time too closely ever to ride over to the park and feed the ducks.

"I told him I had places to go to—you know, like going to see poor old Cousin Dora out in that rest home—and he said anytime I needed him to call and ask for driver 59."

Stacy looked closer at her. Liz was a sly one for all the bland innocence of her rosy face, and she was incurably romantic. Stacy couldn't have her getting any false ideas. "Yes, I used to know Bruce. But I never see him anymore. The last time I saw him he told me if he ever wanted to see me he knew where I lived. I'm surprised he even remembered me."

"He has things weighing on his mind," Liz said.

She, Stacy, must make herself work harder at forgetting. Bruce had certainly been successful at it.

On Friday evening Stacy watched each small passenger leave the station wagon with a pang of regret. She said nothing to anyone about *not* seeing him or her on Monday until she made her last stop for Walter. And then for some reason she was moved to say, "Good-bye, Walter. I won't see you again."

His cap went up a bare half inch over his eyes. "Why?"

"Because Gwen is coming back."

"*Her,*" he said only. He looked at Stacy, looked past her, and said through tight lips, "When I get a little bigger I'm going to beat my big brother to a pulp." He lowered his cap and trudged to his own door. Finding it locked, he turned toward the neighbor's.

She said her good-byes to Donna and Tammie. Donna paid her for the five days and again voiced her warm appreciation. "If I wasn't fully staffed, Stacy, I'd love to have you work with us." She had told Stacy before that three assistants were all she could afford.

Donna drove her home. Stacy walked through the picket gate. *Help wanted female, here I come/Right back where I started from.*

20 ❧

T_{HE} same old discouragement met Stacy's eye when she turned to the want ads the next morning: "PBX Optr"; "Dicta-typist"; "Salad Woman" —for goodness' sake! Her eyes halted at one. "Mod-mod-mod Models. If you are a doll . . ." Oh, no, she had bit on one similar to that before.

She phoned in answer to one that promised a good future and "No exp nec." It turned out to be door-to-door selling of cosmetics. She encircled one: "Recep in med clinic. Pers intv only."

She dressed and took the bus to the personal interview. She had to wait an hour for it at the medical clinic. The interview itself didn't last long. A very capable middle-aged woman took one look at her and said, "I'm sorry, Miss, you're too young."

"I'm eighteen."

"You look about sixteen. People who come to see doctors feel more confidence in someone— Oh, in their twenties at least."

She was walking the four blocks from the bus line to

Hubbell Street when a car driven by a girl who had graduated from St. Jude's passed. Recognizing Stacy, she backed up to say, "Hi there, Bernadette. What are you up to?"

"Getting turned down from jobs mostly."

"Hey, I heard of a job I'll bet you could get," the girl said. "It's at that big Voyager Motel. You know, where airplane passengers stay overnight when they can't make connections to where they're going. They need drivers to get them from the airport and back. They hire boys and girls both. That'd be right up your alley, Stacy. Only you'd have to drive there to work. There's no bus running within a mile of it."

Stacy thanked her and trudged on. A block from home she met Liz going to the Boulevard to pick up a pair of shoes she had left to be repaired. "I'll look around at the dime store and stop in at Pearl's Bakery. Did you get the job?"

"No, but I'm going to take the car and drive out and see about another one."

But Stacy didn't drive out. Instead she had a bitter fight with Ben about using the car. It was parked at the curb, and he was tinkering with the lock on the trunk. She relayed to him the information the girl had given her.

"So I need to take the car. Right away."

"I need it myself."

"You're not working today. What do you need it for?"

She scarcely listened to his explanation, which had to do with the cement job his crew had finished last evening twenty miles out of town. The foreman was worried that a local hailstorm might have damaged it. "I told him I'd swing by and pick him up."

"Doesn't he have a car? Why can't he swing by and pick you up?"

Because the foreman lived on the way to where they were going, Ben said. Because it would be an accommodation to him.

"Aren't you the thoughtful one about accommodating him! Big-hearted Ben. Pardon me, for even thinking this old clunker was the family car. Goodness, no. Nobody else has any right to it but Ben."

His blue eyes flashed ominously. "I don't see *nobody else* putting out dough for brake lining or paying for gas and oil. I don't see your *nobody else* driving Mom to work every night. So you want to tear off on a wild-goose chase to see about a job somebody heard about. If you got it, how'd you ever get out there and back?"

"Not with any help from you. You don't care whether I get a job or not. You'd like to see me sitting around twiddling my thumbs for the rest of my life."

"Don't talk like an imbecile. If you could ever make up your alleged mind what you want to do or be— Haven't Mom and I kept te'ling you we could work it out someway for you to go to college?"

"That's for brains like you. Go on, go on, Benny boy, and accommodate everybody you know. Don't worry about me."

Ben drove off. Stacy banged herself through the gate. She stumbled over a rake with a broken handle that one of the littles must have left lying there. Picking it up, she flung it viciously toward the fence, and got a sliver in the fleshy part of her thumb as the splintered end of the rake left her hand.

Her throat already dry from her walk from the bus was even drier with fury toward Ben. With her unslivered hand she yanked open the door of the refrigerator for the pitcher containing tea ready to be iced. There was only a tablespoonful left in it. Still with her good hand, she filled the teakettle and put it on the gas.

She had to use a needle to get out the splinter. Her shaky hand did a poor job of it. She found the bottle of peroxide and carried it upstairs to her room to get a cotton ball with which to daub it on. In putting the cap back on the bottle, it dropped out of her fingers, bounced onto the dressing table and then into the wastebasket.

Impatiently she rooted through the small collection of wadded-up tissues, hair combings, and the box a bottle of shampoo had come in. Pulling them aside to locate the bottle cap at the bottom, she stared in wide-eyed disbelief. Could miracles still happen?

The bottom of the wicker wastebasket was jagged, with the rough ends of the wicker pushing up like the loose threads on the back of needlework. And there, held down by a corner under a protruding end of wicker, was a card covered by smudges of lipstick.

With no thought of the bottle cap, Stacy pulled it loose, and tenderly rubbed at the smears with a tissue. She came out with a pinkish streaked card, but the printing showed underneath. She carried it to the light of the window and made out:

THE PINK FLAMINGO
AT GREENMONT

Thirty Miles, Thirty Minutes from Denver

Inspired Gourmet Cuisine • *Elegant Decor*
And Even More—Nightly Entertainment

The scrawled signature, Mike, would have been hard to read. But that she remembered.

She stood holding it—her ticket to paradise—breathing light and fast. She threw back her head and laughed in exultant joy—and, yes, in revenge. A lot she cared whether bossy old Ben hit the ceiling or not. Let him, let him wham his head hard on it. She'd show him she didn't have to go crawling to him to get her hands on the wheel of a car. She took a gloating moment to visualize herself purring down Hubbell Street in a car that put *his* beat-up old Chevvy to shame.

And Claire was so right in saying that it was just as well Stacy hadn't found the card the day after graduation. Today the time was miraculously right. No having to soft-soap Mother: she was in Bannon. Ben was on his way to a spot far out on the highway to check on his precious cement job.

And Liz. Liz's strolls to the Boulevard always took a couple of hours by the time she visited with the shoe-repair man and talked with the clerks in the dime store. She'd be even longer in Pearl's Bakery. If Pearl didn't offer her coffee, she would "take the weight off her feet," by stopping at Downey's Drug and sipping it leisurely from a paper cup. Even the littles were gone.

She didn't know where—or care. It was another God-sent miracle—this having an empty house for her phone call to Mike.

She remembered then the teakettle she had put on. But who wanted to waste time making iced tea? She raced down the stairs, gripping tight her ticket to heaven, and turned off the gas burner.

She set herself at the hall telephone and asked the operator for the number on the card. Someone else answered, and she asked for Mike.

The curt jerky voice she remembered announced, "Mike speaking."

"This is Stacy Belford. Do you remember me? You talked to me out at Guido's Gay Nineties on St. Patrick's Day night. And you said you could give me a job. You said I'd be—"

"What experience have you had in this kind of work?"

"Well, not much. But don't you remember you heard me sing, and you said—it was when I sang 'When Irish Eyes Are Smiling'—and you said—"

"Wait a minute, wait a minute. Are you the little redhead with the skin like a rose? I remember. I remember now. Yeh, I can put you on."

"I didn't phone before because I—"

"You called at just the right time. Saturday night is our big night, full and running over. And one of the girls just quit. Didn't I tell you? They get rich so quick they up and leave us."

"I could come right away. Is there a bus to Greenmont?"

"Hold it." He held a brief conversation with someone at his end of the line. "You don't need to take the bus. I'm sending our car down for supplies. We cater to a luxury trade. I'll have Packy swing by for you. He's leaving right away."

"Oh." *Thirty miles—thirty minutes.* "Oh," she repeated, already in her mind racing up the stairs to throw whatever clothes she needed into the striped Mexican tote bag. "What sort of dress do you want me to wear?"

"No worry there. We provide the costume. And it's a humdinger. Had them made specially for the Pink Flamingo."

He hung up before she had time to ask him what sort of songs his luxury trade preferred. She sang out joyously, "I can't type forty-five wpm/but I can sing/I can sing. . . ."

That reminded her. She would take that book of Mother's called *Songs We Sing.* It gave the words and music to about every song anyone had ever heard of. She could refresh herself on the words on the ride to Greenmont with Packy. She had quite a hunt through the sheet music under the seat of the piano bench and through the bigger stack on the piano before she found it.

She'd take her guitar too. She had to dust off the cover and work with a bent buckle to fasten it. She raced back upstairs to gather up her nightclothes and toilet articles.

She would leave a note for the family on the black-

board they called the Idiot Board. The white chalk
wavered in her excited fingers:

*I got a super job not very far out of town. They
need me right away to sing tonight. Will phone
more soon.*

And then for Ben's sake, she crowded in: "It pays so
well I can buy a car of my own."

She was just signing her name when Cully ran barking to the front door. She opened it to see a heavy-set
man with opaque brown eyes set in a swarthy scarred
face. "Are you the girl Mike told me to bring? I'll take
your bag."

Stacy, the guitar under one arm, her pouch purse
hooked over her other wrist, almost raced to the car
she was so eager to be off and away from Hubbell
Street before any of the family returned.

Packy made two stops in the downtown district. The
first was at a wholesale fish market from which he
emerged with several cartons giving out a fishy odor.
"Shrimp," he said almost unnecessarily. The second
stop was at a produce house where he picked up a flat
carton of avocadoes and another of what looked to
Stacy like some sort of small squash. "Papayas," he enlightened her.

He was most untalkative. Stacy would have liked to
ask questions about the Pink Flamingo, but he kept his
eyes on the road, weaving the long dark car deftly in
and out of traffic. He skirted the small town of Green-

mont and turned off the main highway. He took still another sharp turn where a road sign directed with a bright pink hand: THE PINK FLAMINGO.

Stacy was too agog to notice many details about her new place of employment. She saw only that it was a widespread pink adobe building of the Spanish type. Her driver stopped in front, leaving the motor running, and made the longest comment he had made yet: "I'll let you in before I take my load around to the kitchen side. Place don't open till six. About five now."

They walked up a white graveled pathway bordered by real or artificial shrubs set in wooden tubs. Stacy thought fleetingly of Liz's lemon tree the nice taxi driver had deposited by their piano.

I used to know a boy named Bruce Seerie a long time ago.

Strings of red peppers hung on either side of the heavy door Packy unlocked. He called out, "Mike, you there?" and hearing an answer, said, "Go ahead," and closed the door behind her.

Clutching Mexican bag and purse, and with the guitar under one arm, she looked around unseeingly until her eyes became accustomed to the dimmer light after the bright sunshine outside. She was in a lounge with a piano and a bar at one end. The dining room was beyond. She was only vaguely aware of walls decorated with palm trees and great pink-feathered birds.

A light was turned on over the piano, so that its pink glow fell on the keys. A man sat at it with his hands on them—a man with sad eyes and drooping jowls. And then Stacy saw the dark fidgety form of the man who stood between the piano and bar. Ah, there was Mike who had told her she sang like a nightingale.

She had a feeling she was interrupting an unpleasant scene, for Mike was saying with an angry outjutting of jaw, "Okay, okay, so you came early to try out some numbers. Okay, just stick to the piano and stay away from the bar." The piano player pretended not to hear but trailed his fingers softly over the keys.

Three jerky bounds brought Mike beside her. "Glad you got here. Marge tells me the reservations are pouring in. Just a minute." He turned to a desk with a cash register and fumbled through some shelves behind it and brought out a white page. "Just a matter of form. Have to get your signature on the dotted line."

"I brought my guitar. I can chord on it. Some songs sound a lot better with it."

He didn't answer that. He shoved the paper at her. "Guess I'd better give you a little light. One customer said you needed a seeing-eye dog in here. Fill in your name, age, date. I'll run through the fine print for you." It told what the Pink Flamingo would pay her an hour. "Doesn't sound like much, but the tips are what count. And how. And the more smiles, the bigger and better."

She signed the paper, putting down her age as eighteen because she would be eighteen next month, and why quibble and say seventeen and eleven months and three days?

Someone tried the locked door. Mike stiffened and waited. Then he moved swiftly not to the door but to a draperied window and peered out warily. "Tourists," he muttered. "They can wait in the car till six."

He turned back to Stacy. "I'll show you where to go to get into your toggery."

He didn't offer to carry either bag or guitar but led the way through the maze of tables in the dining room. Pink-jacketed busboys were setting them with china, glass, and silver. There were pink cloths on the tables too. Already food smells were filtering out from wherever the kitchen was located.

And Mike kept tossing back jerky sentences over his shoulder as he hurried along. "We have quarters for the staff right under the same roof. Oh, yes, all the comforts home never had. You'll like the girls. We don't put up with grouches. Here you are."

They were in a narrow hall with two doors on either side. "Just go in that first door. I forget which girl you'll share the room with. Marge will be around to fix you up." His eyes raked over her. "About a size ten. But like they say, one size fits all. Marge will fill you in, too. It goes slow at first, so you won't have any trouble. The big bang starts around ten."

He was gone. She realized then that he hadn't said a word about her singing. He hadn't even introduced her to the sad-eyed man at the piano. Haltingly she opened the door.

The room was small with two narrow beds in it, one of the beds looking most untidy with tumbled clothes and a half-eaten cinnamon roll on it. A girl was standing in front of the mirror opposite the door putting on false eyelashes.

It was her costume—if such it could be called—that held Stacy in both shock and horror. The girl was encased in a leotard of gaudy pink mesh, cut low in the neck and sleeveless. Over it was a skirt—if such it could be called—of feathery plumage. The feathers at the back of the skirt were bunchier and perkier, intended to resemble a bird's tail, no doubt.

Stacy breathed inwardly Gran O'Byrne's favorite expression, "The saints preserve us!" The skin-tight mesh showed up the girl's long legs, a little too fleshy through the thighs. The legs ended in gold slippers with purple heels. She looked for all the world like one of Gran O'Byrne's half-grown, half-fledged turkeys.

Stacy's horrified eyes met the eyes of the girl in the mirror. She had dropped her fingers from the left eye with its fastened-on lash. A wondering unbelieving smile—a glowing familiar smile of friendliness and love —lit up her face as she turned to face her. "Stacy, as I live and breathe! For land sakes, what are you doing here?"

It was Allegra who was standing there with one eye heavily shadowed by the glued-on eyelash and the other with only its meager natural fringe. Stacy's mind took a quick leap back to that drizzly afternoon when she and Allegra had sat in Schmitty's, and of Allegra in between bites of her corned-beef sandwich telling her about the super job she was waiting for—a job where the tips were folding money.

Allegra repeated, "What are you doing here?"

Stacy didn't answer that, but muttered in a stunned voice, "Then this must be the place you said the police closed down?"

"That's right. Because the waitresses were topless.

All the people at Greenmont got up a petition or whatever you call it. So Mike came through with this
crummy outfit. He copied it from something he saw in
a Broadway musical, he said. We're the Flamingo
Girls."

"It's obscene," Stacy said flatly.

At that, the door behind her opened, and a girl,
older than either Allegra or Stacy and already dressed
in her clinging pink mesh and feathery skirt, came in
with a businesslike click of heels. Her eyes raked criti-
cally over Stacy's figure. "Yes, this one should fit like
skin."

She shook out the short skirt that looked something
like an Indian war bonnet and dropped it on the un-
cluttered bed. She tossed a pink garment that could
have been taken for an elongated pair of panty hose
beside it. "Allegra, give her the pumps that other girl
left." She glanced again at the rooted figure of Stacy
still clutching the guitar and striped bag, and said
crisply, "Don't be wasting time, you two. Let's not get
Mike riled up," and went out the door.

"That's Marge," Allegra said. "She's the hostess.
Hard as nails but honey-sweet to Mike."

Stacy burst out, "I won't wear it. When I saw Mike
—he was at Guido's and he heard me sing, and he said
I'd be a knockout. He said I sang like a nightingale.
That's why I came. That's why I brought the guitar."

Allegra listened with a rueful shaking of her head.
"Aw, lambie, it was your smile and your cute figure he
was thinking of—it wasn't your singing. He worked
that gag on another girl named Norma, but when she
came, she had to sling hash with the rest of us—"

"But it says right on the card nightly entertainment."

"That means Harry at the piano. Oh, sure, maybe way late at night some drunk old codger may want somebody to sing some song his mother used to. But nobody'd have to have a voice like a nightingale—"

"I won't stay here. I won't wear that—those pink tights and that silly feathered shift. I couldn't stand it."

"No, you couldn't," Allegra said, shaking her head again. "And there's a lot more you couldn't stand: the talk you have to take, and the pawers—and the pinching your behind. Gracious, sometimes mine is black and blue. But I don't mind. I just go on grinning and thinking about when I quit. No, don't stay, Stacy. You get out right away. Did Mike have you sign anything?"

"Yes, a paper. He said it was just a matter of form."

Allegra considered that a moment. "You leave anyway. Only don't let Mike see you. He can be hell on wheels. I'll show you how to get out the back door. Then you hoof it over to where the Pink Flamingo sign is, and somebody—there're a lot of farmers around here—will give you a lift to Greenmont. You got enough money for bus fare back?"

Stacy nodded. "Allegra, you come too. Don't stay here where you get pinched and have to fight off the pawers."

"No, not yet." Her beatific smile lighted up both her shadowed and her unshadowed eye. "I'm going to stick out maybe two weeks more—maybe only one if I'm lucky on tips. Because I heard from Robbie. He was wounded in Vietnam, and now he's in a hospital in San Francisco."

"Does he want you to come out?"

Allegra laughed joyously. "You know what he said on a postcard? 'Why don't you try San Francisco's invigorating climate?' I told him I would, and he's looking for me. I'm going to fly. It won't cost too much more than a bus—and it's a lot quicker. I've got almost enough. I mean, I'll have to have something to live on when I get there and be able, you know, to take him presents like books and peanuts. He always used to buy me peanuts and eat most of them himself. I can hardly wait."

This time there was a peremptory rat-a-tat on the door. Marge's voice warned, "Five minutes, girls."

Allegra moved to the door and listened until the click of heels faded. She opened it and stepped out. "The other girls are gone," she whispered hurriedly. "Mike wanted them to help with special decorations in the party room. Come on. I'll show you the way."

She tiptoed her way down another narrow hall cluttered by cleaning equipment and mop buckets. Stacy tiptoed after her. Allegra slid a bolt off the door and opened it.

"Go on, Stacy," she urged. "Packy will be on the other side in the parking lot. Go on, while everybody's busy in the party room. If you see Jake, tell him I've almost got it made. Go on now, Stacy. Lots of luck."

Stacy's last glimpse was of Allegra in the feathered bustle looking for all the world as she scuttled off like one of Gran's long-legged turkeys running for shelter.

21 ✑

M *OVING* away from the back door, Stacy rounded one of the jutting pink stucco wings of the building. She was looking about confusedly for the road Packy had come on, when she saw a car come swerving down the spur of the dirt road with sure intent. Then that would be the direction to take to the more traveled one. But she would be unable to reach it without going to the front of the building because the field at the side which she might have cut across was fenced. She followed the narrow walk, wishing she wasn't so loaded down with tote bag and guitar and that the sun wasn't still so bright in the sky.

She reached the wider flagstone path with its border of potted shrubs that led to the front door. Then she had to step aside onto the finely ground oystershell for a party of diners. It was evidently their car she had seen, it had been turned over to Packy to park. Minute chunks of the white shell became lodged between the soles of her sandals and her bare feet, but she couldn't stop now to shake them out, not until she had put some distance between herself and the Pink Flamingo.

She heard the front door opening for the guests. Dear heaven, she hoped it wasn't Mike, the genial host, who had opened it. She didn't glance back, but hurried on.

She hadn't gone far down the dirt road when she heard a shout of "Hold on there!" behind her. Mike had seen her. She kept on, even though she heard his footsteps gaining on her. The hand that grasped her arm wrenched her sideways, and the voice was teasing but with iron in it too. "Now where do you think you're going, little girl?"

She planted her feet as firmly as she could with the splintery shell pinching them. "I'm going home. I won't wear that silly—that filthy outfit." Her voice turned squeaky, "I thought you wanted me to sing."

"I do. Of course, I do. But didn't I tell you you'd have to lend a hand with the tables? Everyone does. I do myself. Who wants singing until their stomachs are full? You just come on back. We'll talk it over. You can't rush off like this. I've got your name on a contract."

He tugged her farther to the side of the road because of an approaching car. This car didn't pass but ground to a stop. It wasn't a shiny capable car, such as one of Mike's luxury trade would be apt to drive, but a rattly weathered brown one even older than the hard-used Belford Chevvy.

The sidewise flip and the wild thumping of Stacy's heart told her who the driver was even before he thrust himself out of the car. He was wearing the same gray denim shirt and slacks, but this evening no cab driver's cap hid his black mat of hair. He came around the hood of the car and said curtly, "I've come to take you home, Stacy."

She was incapable of answering. This sudden appearance of Bruce Seerie was too incomprehensible.

But Mike was capable of answering, and now it was all iron in his voice. "She's not leaving. I didn't drag her here. *She* phoned me. *She* asked for the job. Okay, so I send a driver in for her. Okay, so she don't like the outfit the girls wear. She wants to stand up and sing like Jenny Lind. So she's walking out on the job. Only she signed a contract to stay for two months, *unless*— it's right there in print—*unless* there's justifiable cause for leaving. Okay?"

"It's not okay. She's got justifiable cause for leaving. She's not eighteen yet. You want to let go her arm or you want me to report it to the police in Greenmont and have them swoop down on you?"

Mike shifted his never still, black eyes on Stacy. "You said you were eighteen," he accused. "I remember asking you."

"I will be next month," she said thinly. "I didn't think just that little bit would make any difference."

With a venomous snort of disgust and defeat, he dropped her arm as though it were hot. Without another word he went off with his jerky stride down the short span of road to the hulk of pink adobe.

And still Stacy stood in a confused hodgepodge of hows and whys. She asked the foremost *how*. "How did you know where I was?"

"Liz told me. She got in touch with me to ask if I knew anything about a place called the Pink Flamingo."

"Oh." Then in her flurry of excitement and getting ready, she must have left Mike's card—maybe on the phone stand, maybe on the piano bench. "What did you say?"

"I told her, Yes, I knew about the Flamingo. I've driven people out here from Denver. And I've also come out on call and had to go in for customers and pour them into the taxi. So come on."

But he had no smile for her. If only he'd say, "Remember, I always wanted to shelter you from all turmoil and that's why I came." He acted like someone who had been sent to do a job and wanted to get it over and done with.

"Did Liz ask—or maybe beg—you to come up and get me? I suppose you didn't want to, but—"

A car stopped on the road behind them, its way blocked by Bruce's car and the two of them standing beside it. The toot of the horn was a request for room to pass.

Bruce took the guitar and the striped tote bag from her and shoved both in the back of the car. He opened the front door for her. "Get in," he said with a quirk of lips that still wasn't a smile. "It's my car—all mine such as it is and with no strings attached. Get in. We're blocking Mike's supper trade."

She got in. He gave his whole attention to driving on and gauging the space in front of the parking lot to make a turn. She gave hers to taking off first one sandal and then the other, and whacking the gravelly shell out of them. By that time they were off the dirt road and onto the paved one.

"Look, Bruce, as long as Liz put the bee on you and you couldn't help yourself—I mean, as long as you were *forced* into coming after me, you don't have to drive me back. Just let me off at Greenmont, and I'll take the bus."

She waited for him to say, "I wasn't forced into coming. I came because I wanted to."

"I told Liz I'd bring you home," he said and took the turn onto the highway that skirted Greenmont. He drove on steadily but with far less speed than he usually did. "I've got a slow leak in that front tire on your side. But it ought to last—it's only about twenty miles till I get to the edge of town. A fellow I know named Hal works in a filling station there. Can you feel it give?"

In her wrought-up state she couldn't tell whether the tire under her had give to it or solidity. They rode on at what seemed a snail's pace with car after car whizzing past them.

"Might help, Stacy," he said, "if you climbed into the backseat, so's to take a little weight off it. Sit on my side behind me. You can do it without my stopping, can't you?"

Feeling more than ever like excess baggage, she clambered over the front seat and into the corner behind him. In this whole crazy disappointing day of being turned down for a job and fighting with Ben and fleeing from the Pink Flamingo, this was the crowning humiliation of all—for Bruce to have been sent after her by a worried and insistent Liz, as though she were an adventurous pup that had strayed too far from home and had to be picked up and brought back.

On the outskirts of Denver he turned off the highway and slowly wound his way through streets of little old houses with fancy trim and well-kept yards. He pulled into a filling station on a corner. "Made it," he muttered more to himself than to her with a sigh of relief.

His friend Hal was filling a gas tank. After a dash into the small office to get change for the car owner, he hurried over to Bruce and the car. Heck, yes, he could fix the tire in ten–fifteen minutes if business would just slack up long enough. "I'm here alone. Bud had to go out to charge a battery. But I'll jack her up, and we'll—" Another car drove in for gas.

"Give me the jack, and I'll do it," Bruce offered.

Stacy got out of the car while he raised the front end a half foot off the cement. He removed the wheel and rolled it into the garage behind the station. The evening sun still beamed brightly. She sought a small blob of shade by a stack of new tires that gave off a strong rubbery smell through their brown wrappings. Her hair felt hot on her neck and shoulders. She twisted it into a coil that didn't stay for as long as the time it took to twist it.

Her eyes followed Bruce as he went into the office and used the phone on the wall over the water cooler. That figured. Probably letting his date know that he'd been held up. She wondered just how he'd explain his being delayed by a girl he used to know.

Nothing will ever hurt as much as this, as Bruce treating me like the lost dog he was delegated to pick up and deliver home. Please God, let me get through it without letting him know I care. Let me play it cool, as though I had done as good a job of forgetting as he has.

He came out of the office and stopped at the cold-drink container. "Out of Cokes," he called to her. "You want an orange or this green one that's lime-something?"

"Either one." And when he put the opened bottle in her hand, she said as politely as though they were strangers, "Thanks a lot," and took a long drink of it.

"I suppose you're hungry," he said almost belligerently. "But I can't even buy you a hot dog till I see whether I'll need a new inner tube or not."

"Don't let it worry you."

He fidgeted beside her while he watched Hal cleaning a windshield. "I wish that other fellow would get here, so we could fix up the tire. You in a hurry to get home?"

She couldn't keep the desolation out of her voice. "No, I'm in no hurry to have Ben lace me up one side and down the other. I wish I never had to go home. If I knew of anywhere to go to, I'd start running."

He gave her an odd look. "I thought maybe you'd want to go running to that soul of devotion Allegra told me about. The one that was Johnny-on-the-spot at your play and that sent you flowers."

The words tumbled out before she could stop them. "That's more than you did. You didn't even come with Jake and Allegra. She said—"

Heavens, she must watch herself more closely.

"Did you expect me to?" he challenged.

"I'd have been a fool if I had. As the Irishman says after he's been kicked downstairs three times, 'I can take a hint as good as the next one.'" The airy laugh she had intended came out with a catch in it. "Why would I expect you when you all but threw me out of the basement that day? I don't blame you though. I guess it stuck in your craw because I called you a donkey that—"

"I'll tell you what stuck in my craw," he hurled out. "It was my making a jackass out of myself at the Student Union. Slopping down that 'lacquered' punch, as you would say, and getting sick as a billy goat and then—then—"

"I always wondered if you made it in time."

"Just barely." Still with pent-up emotion he threw the words out at her. "Then you had to come that day when I'd had a bellyful of everyone I knew shoving in with their jawing and poor-Brucing and telling me what to do and what not to do. All right, I *was* a heel, and that stuck in my craw too if it makes you feel any better."

He gave her a look as though he'd said more than he intended. And then with the desperation of one who now feels he might as well say more, he continued, "And I'll tell you why I didn't go to see you playing the lead in your school play. That was the day I tried to enlist, not that I see any sense in all that mess in Vietnam, but I'd have gone anyplace to get away— away from it all, as the old cliché goes—and that's when—you'll laugh at this—I didn't pass the physical."

She didn't laugh. "*You* didn't pass the physical?"

"That old football knee. I told them all I had to do was tape it up tight, and I didn't know I had it. But they still wouldn't take me. So there I was—back to a big fat zero."

"You've got a job driving a taxi. That's more than I have."

"Thuhh! But for how long? Yellow Cab wouldn't hire me because I'm not twenty-one. The Red and White is a little independent outfit, and they only put me on because they needed extra drivers for the conventions this summer. I'll be the first one laid off when they're over. Mom's living for the day when I am. She's afraid some of her friends will see me driving a cab. She thinks if I get hungry enough I'll take that conscience money Dad set up for me to go to law school. That's one thing I'm sure of—about the only thing. I don't know what I want to do or can do, but I know damnwell I'm not going to be a scheming conniving lawyer. And I know damnwell I'll stay right on in what Aunt Vinia called a hog wallow before I'll move back with Mother and have her nipping at my heels."

She had never thought he could be so bitterly vehement. He took a long burbling swallow of orange drink. "All right. Now you've heard the life story of a jerk. Now you tell me something. What made you go dashing off like a halfwit to that gyp joint up there?"

"How did I know it was a gyp joint?" It was a relief somehow to match his belligerence. "From what Mike said I thought he wanted me to sing—maybe to *help* wait on tables—but mostly to sing. Why do you think I lugged up the guitar? And then I saw Allegra. She works there, and—"

"I know. But Allegra isn't you."

Jake had said something the same thing: "She's one of the pure in heart that the Bible tells us are the blessed. That gal can go through the slime and filth of the world and come out loving and untouched. Something like a duck that sheds water."

"And then a girl brought in the outfit I was to wear. You never saw such a horrible—"

"I've seen them," he grunted. "Sexy. Mike saw to that."

"So Allegra helped me to leave through the back door. I wanted her to come too, but she wants to make more money to go out to Robbie in San Francisco."

"Yeh. She told Jake and me about it."

Bruce's friend Hal was suddenly beside them. "Bud's here now. And the patch—that's all it needed—is setting. You'll soon be able to roll."

His interruption brought them back to where they were and why. Engrossed in their accusations and self-defense, they had forgotten they were in a noisy smelly filling station. They had lashed out at each other in the old days. Those fights had always been because of his resentment over her friendly outgoingness and her resentment of his dominating parents. The parting in January, which was *almost* the battle to end all battles, had happened because of her weary disillusionment in him.

This was different. This sparring under a cover of

anger and defiance was really a probing, a seeking, a longing, to find out what was in the heart of the other. The real words that pride held back were, Did you forget me? Do you still care?

Hal added, "Now that Bud's back, I'm off. You mind if I ride in as far as the U with you? It's Saturday night, and I got a girl there I want to see."

"Come right along," Bruce said.

He replaced the wheel with many thumps and bangs while Hal got ready. It was when Bruce took out his wallet to pay for the job that with the money a slip of folded paper appeared. "Stacy, I forgot all about giving you this message. Liz read it to me over the phone. Doesn't make much sense to me, but she said it probably would to you."

Stacy unfolded the paper and read: "Gwen staying on in Calif. Phone Donna at Appleseed soon as poss." She read it twice. *Gwen staying on in Calif.* It might mean she was staying for only another week. It might mean—please, God—that she wasn't coming back. And if that was so, Stacy would be permanently hired. She could even take courses that would make her more competent as a day nursery assistant. She, Stacy Belford, would have a goal to work toward.

"Let's go," Bruce was saying with great impatience.

Hal stepped back from the car door he was holding open. He grinned at her and said, "Lucky you. You get to sit between us two playboys."

22 ❧

$O_{N\ T\ H\ E}$ ride from the filling station
to the university in south Denver, the boys carried on
the conversation alone. It was mostly about the new
transmission Bruce's car needed and how much it
would cost and when Hal would be able to do the
work.

Bruce stopped at the corner of the campus, and Hal
got out. The car waited for the traffic light to change.

*Only eight or nine more blocks to go, and then I'll
get out and say, "Thanks a lot, Bruce," and he'll go
speeding on to his date. Finish.*

Just to make conversation, she asked, "How is Aunt
Vinia?"

"Fine. She'd like me to come and stay with her. She
calls that one bedroom my room—"

"Why don't you?"

Again there was challenging defiance in his voice
and in the way he stepped on the gas and shot across
the Boulevard on the green light. "Because she'd baby
me, that's why. I got bossed at home, but when I

stayed with her she always coddled me. She'd do it now. She'd slip me a few bucks if she thought I was short. I've got this one shirt and pair of pants that I wash out at night and iron after a fashion. She'd go rushing out and buy me more."

She didn't answer, and he went on. "I'm working at not being a weakling and a moocher. I mooched on Jake for awhile. But now I don't. He pays the rent out of his G.I., but I work out my share by repairing that cabin of his. I'm better at it than he is. He gets an idea of putting in a Dutch door or a skylight, but he doesn't have a clue how to go about it. I have to get to Sears before it closes to pick up some hardware to take up there tomorrow."

"What time does it close?"

"Eight thirty. I phoned from the filling station to find out."

"Oh!" she breathed, and then another, "Oh!"

So it wasn't a girl he had phoned to tell her he was held up. It wasn't a girl he was thinking of when he tapped his foot so impatiently and muttered, "I wish that other fellow would get here." She couldn't hold back the words any longer. "I tried to forget you, Bruce, but I couldn't."

He answered slowly without looking at her, "I couldn't forget you either—not if I lived to be a hundred. I tried—I tried booze and girls." And suddenly he was talking fast as though the floodgates were open. "I didn't tell you enough back there at the filling station. The reason I slugged down that punch at the Student Union was to get up nerve to corner you and tell you—"

"What did you want to tell me?"

"That I wasn't the carrot following the donkey. You spoiled that car of Mom's for me that I thought I had to have to get to basketball games. And then I wanted to tell you—I hadn't told anyone else about seeing Dad with his sweetie and his hugging that little kid. Sure, I yelled at you to get out. God's sake, Stacy, do you think I wanted you to see me break down and bawl like a baby? And the reason I didn't come to your play was because I was lower than a snake's belly"—again that quirk of lips that wasn't a smile—"I learned that phrase from you. And I was afraid I'd take a poke at the boy friend who knows what he wants and goes after it. That's a lot more than I do."

They had reached Hubbell Street by now. He didn't stop outside the Belfords' picket gate but drove on to stop at the next corner where the willow tree stood with its full drooping branches. There it was again— that pull like a magnet between them. She said, "Bruce, hold my hand."

He gripped her outstretched hand in both of his and pressed it hungrily. His hands were leaner and harder and calloused from much gripping of a car wheel and from his work on Jake's cabin. But there it was again— that same all's-right-with-the-world feeling. Her hand felt as though it had come home.

"I want to tell you something, Bruce. The very first time I saw you when I was coming down the walk—"

"Bouncing a basketball. I remember."

"Yes, and you showed me how to shoot baskets. You

brought me that smelly lotion for my charley horse. We'd sit at Downey's—and I thought that you were stronger and more of a man than any boy I ever knew. I always felt so safe and protected—"

"You told me all that before," he interrupted.

"No, wait, wait. I have to tell you the rest. The reason I fought with you and said such hateful things—I mean, it wasn't *that* you I said them to. It was the stranger that sort of bobbed up—"

"The donkey following the carrot. You told me that too," he said harshly.

"Let me finish. When I saw you at the Student Union you were a stranger too. And that day in Jake's basement—"

"You don't have to rub it in. I know what an unwashed heel I was that day."

"Wait till I finish. Then when you brought in Liz's lemon tree that day you weren't a stranger anymore. You were the Bruce I had looked up to and been so wild about. Only you looked at me that day as if I was a stranger. You even told Liz you *used* to know me." One large tear splashed down on his enclosing hand. "Don't you want me to be your girl again?"

His hand tightened on her. "I want you—I'll always want you." Again the rasping bitterness tinged his words. "But what I've been trying to tell you is that I'm—that you'd be better off with your hero. I'm a mess. Jake's right when he says I'm the chicken fresh out of the shell. I'm still scared, Stacy, and I don't know where I'm going. I know what I don't want—I told you that. I used to think it was hogwash—all that talk about somebody not being able to find himself. But that's me."

"Me too. This whole summer has been awful because I couldn't find anything I could do until—" But some feminine wisdom kept her from telling him that the door had opened a crack for her.

"That day I drove Liz home, I was telling her that I never knew I could hammer a nail in straight until I worked on that falling-down cabin of Jake's. I like sawing wood and making doors fit. Sometimes I sit in that dismal hole of Jake's and imagine myself building a house from the ground up. And Liz told me to get a job with a builder and take courses at the university in architecture. But right now I haven't got the guts to let go the taxi job. Not until I'm fired, I suppose. Because —well, a fellow gets scared of being hungry."

"Did you ever figure out what to do with the can of water chestnuts?"

"I just opened the can and ate them as was—and drank the juice. They were pretty awful and not even filling."

"Bruce, you don't have to be hungry. Anytime you come to our house—"

"No," he fairly yelled. "No. I'm trying to tell you that I have to bumble this out on my own." And then more gently, he said, "That's what I'm afraid of. I can't ask you to be my girl—not yet. I'm not anywhere near the man you thought I was. I'd lean on you."

"I wouldn't baby you like Aunt Vinia."

"I'd still lean on you. You're so giving. I'd spill out

all my poison on you. I still can't forgive Dad—or Mom either for being so vindictive toward him. She's still putting the screws on him. I have mean hateful times when I have either to hurt people or to fight with them. I'd take it out on you. Maybe you can't understand—I can't myself."

"Yes—yes, I can," she faltered.

"Not yet, Stacy. Just give me time."

They were interrupted. Jill was standing at the picket gate and bellowing at them. They could catch enough of the words to know it was something about Liz keeping Stacy's dinner warm for hours.

Even then he didn't unclasp her hand.

And now Matt added his bellow to Jill's. He made a tunnel of his hands and shouted through them, "Liz said to tell Bruce to come in too."

"Good old Liz," he said. "Tell her about the hinges and window glass I have to get. I'll just about make it."

Slowly their hands parted. He helped her out of the car. He carried the Mexican tote bag and the guitar, and walked with her to the gate. Again the gentle twang as he handed the guitar to her. He said with a near smile, "I won't come when I'm my meanest self. But maybe sometime when I'm dead beat—"

"Come anytime, Bruce."

He turned toward the car on the corner, and she walked through the gate. And then with her hampering load, she came running back. "Bruce, wait—" she called. They met halfway between the gate and the willow tree. "I just wanted to tell you. I'll start saving our dry bread, and when you come by, we'll go over and feed the ducks. It's been so long—our little ducks must be starvelous."

That brought a low chuckle from him. "Lord, lord, Stacy. I've been so starvelous to hear *you* say starvelous." He cupped her face in his two hands and kissed her swiftly even though Jill stood on the back step watching. "That's so you'll remember you're the only girl I've ever cared about."

"Me too. Isn't it crazy?"

She watched him get into the car and drive off. She turned back and walked through the gate. She could take Ben's lacing down now. And why had she thought a car of her own was so all important? It was enough for now to know that Donna at the Appleseed was waiting for her to call. And that someday Bruce would stop, and she would climb in beside him—not into his mother's perfumed car but into a rattly brown one with no strings attached.

ABOUT THE AUTHOR

Lenora Mattingly Weber was the author of more than twenty-two books for young readers, including the popular Beany Malone series. Beany Malone was the first of Mrs. Weber's heroines, but when she finally married the boy next door in *Something Borrowed, Something Blue,* Mrs. Weber introduced Katie Rose Belford and, later, Katie Rose's sister Stacy, the heroine of her final novels *Hello, My Love, Good-Bye* and *Sometimes a Stranger.*

Lenora Mattingly Weber was born in Missouri, but her family left the state when she was twelve to homestead on the Colorado plains. She went to high school in Denver and after graduation married and lived in Denver. Until her death, in January 1971, Mrs. Weber conducted a monthly column in *Extension Magazine* and wrote short stories for America's leading magazines: *The Saturday Evening Post, Ladies' Home Journal, Good Housekeeping,* and *McCall's,* in addition to her writing for young people.

All of Mrs. Weber's manuscripts and papers and copies of the first editions of each of her books were presented to the Denver Public Library in a ceremony in her honor in November 1969. They are now part of the Colorado Authors Collection in the Western History Department of the library.